Other Fish *in the* Sea

Other Fish *in the* Sea

LISA KUSEL

An Imprint of Hyperion
New York

Library of Congress Cataloging-in-Publication Data

Kusel, Lisa
    Other fish in the sea / Lisa Kusel.—1st ed.
      p. cm.
    Contents: Juvenile hall—Prairie dogs—Perdition—Bars—Bones—Craps—Other fish in the sea—Single white female—SWM—The other side.
    ISBN: 0-7868-8802-4
    1. Young women—Fiction. I. Title.

PS3611.U737 O8 2003
813'.6—dc21

2002032941

Hyperion books are available for special promotions and premiums. For details, contact Michael Rentas, Manager, Inventory and Premium Sales, Hyperion, 77 West 66th Street, 11th floor, New York, New York 10023-6298, or call 212-456-0133.

FIRST EDITION

Designed by Lorelle Graffeo

10 9 8 7 6 5 4 3 2 1

For Victor, my forever love

Contents

Other Fish *in the* Sea

Juvenile Hall

A MOTHER'S LOVE MUST break up, fragment, so that all her nestlings get a worm. Helen knew this as surely as she knew which nails she needed to have the manicurist fix next Tuesday when she got back home. Right index, left pinkie, where she'd banged it trying to shove her Louis Vuitton suitcase into the overhead bin while getting no help from the younger people who sat, pretending to read their newspapers, not looking up at her. Helen was infuriated throughout the flight from San Diego to Seattle to visit her daughter, but she said nothing; she sat quietly in her seat and read her *Cosmopolitan*.

A good enough reason to have stayed married to Jerry, having those extra hands for heavy lifting, contractor's hands. They were weak when he walked out three years ago, though, soft and flimsy, hanging there at his sides as he asked her if there was anything she needed before he left for good. It had taken close to forty years for that absurd question to fall from his selfish mouth. *Yes, I'd like to see you crawl over broken glass from our house to your new girlfriend's house,* she wanted to say. Instead she smiled and asked him to make her a cup of coffee.

"What? A cup of coffee?"

"Yes, a cup of coffee. For almost forty years I've been making you coffee, pouring your juice, and buttering your toast. I don't think it's too much to ask to have you make me a cup," she said stiffly, leading him back into the kitchen. She sat up on the stool, pushed her chin down into upturned palms, and leaned her sagging elbows against the counter as she watched him take a cup and saucer—Johnson Bros.' Olde English Countryside pattern—from the cupboard. They'd bought twelve place settings in London a quarter of a century ago. On a whim they'd left the kids with Helen's sister and jetted off to Europe for two weeks, making love in Parisian hotels, holding their hands out to the floating butterflies along the Rhine, dancing on the veranda of a Riviera restaurant, the lights above them dangling, swaying in the wind.

He put a teaspoon of the instant dark grounds into the cup and stared at his feet while the water came slowly to a boil. She was aware that the silence between them now was not so different from the heavy hush that had sat between them at the dining room table for the last few months. No, this was nothing new.

He poured the hot water into the cup and stirred it before looking up at her. Helen was ready for the next words.

"How do you take it?"

After all this time. She thought back to their blind date so many years ago, when, as a seventeen-year-old girl, eager to get out of her parents' house, she agreed to meet the gangly young man who lived three doors over from her second cousin in Flatbush. Jerry was no Romeo, but he was twenty years old and ready to go off to the Korean War. He kissed her bleached blonde hair (still dyed exactly the same color to this day) and promised to write.

Which he did. Twice a week. "Look at the moon at exactly 5:00 P.M. on Saturday," he wrote. "Know that I am seeing it too and seeing your eyes past it. Feeling our hearts beat together."

"Get out," Helen said. And watched him shake his head as he made for the front door.

That was three years ago. During those first months following Jerry's absence, Helen had trouble rousing herself to do much of anything. After drinking her cup of coffee at the breakfast bar, she'd walk the few steps to the living room and stretch out on the chintz couch. With remote in hand, she started two new soap operas and ordered every age-defying lotion and masque QVC sold. Her three children did their best to place solace within arm's reach. Evan, her youngest, stopped by every day after work to see if she needed him to program the VCR or change the oil in her car. Manly activities, the ones Jerry took care of without effort. Brian called and promised to visit, but she knew he wouldn't come soon; the divorce had hit him especially hard. She talked to her middle child, Elly, on the telephone constantly. Helen found comfort in her daughter's gentle voice as Elly prodded her to get out of the house, take a yoga class at the senior center, have lunch with girlfriends.

By the end of that first year Helen slowly—as slowly as the seasons change—realized that she was less lonely by herself than she had been when married to Jerry. "I've had a revelation," she'd told Elly on the telephone. "I'm more comfortable in my own house now than I was when your father lived here."

Elly said, "Hooray for you, *Mamacita*. Now that you're feeling good about yourself, why not go out and spread the wealth?"

They'd laughed together at Elly's not-so-subtle phrase. Helen never thought she would be discussing her sex life with her daughter. Just as she never thought she'd have to come to Elly's rescue because of a man. But here she was in Seattle, doing just that.

Elly was waiting for her at Gate 15 at SeaTac Airport. Helen noticed her daughter's shoulders slumping unnaturally, her eyes wet with tears. "Come here, sweetheart," Helen murmured as the two embraced.

"Thanks for coming, Mom," Elly said. "I feel bad I dragged you up here for such a stupid reason."

"What do you mean, stupid? I'd have come if you'd sprained your ankle," Helen said. She was thrilled that Elly wanted her to be in Seattle with her. They need you through childhood, she mused, but as soon as they become teenagers, children are ready to go the world alone. "I'm very happy you need me."

Elly grabbed Helen's bag and together they walked toward the parking garage. "You and Daddy were married forever," she said. "I was only dating Kevin for a couple of months. I can't believe I let myself get so involved in such a short amount of time."

They got into the car and Elly began to cry the moment she put the key in the ignition. Helen watched her daughter's head bob up and down with the rhythm of her sobs. "Oh, Elly." She unbuckled her seat belt to get out, but Elly stopped her with her hand.

"No, Mom." She sniffed. "No. I'm fine now." She turned the engine on and started driving. Helen took a tissue out of her handbag and handed it to Elly.

"Thanks," she said, wiping her nose and eyes. "It's not like this is the first time I've had my heart broken, right?" she asked the windshield in front of her.

"No, but let's hope it's the last time," Helen said. She smiled a sad and knowing smile at Elly's profile; her normally thick brown hair hung in strands around her sallow face as if it had given up the fight. Helen patted the back of her own coiffed hair and turned and watched the windshield wipers splashing away the raindrops.

After unpacking her sweaters and hanging her slacks in the guest room closet, Helen walked into her daughter's small sunroom overlooking Puget Sound. The clouds were thinning and she hoped the sky would clear long enough for her to glimpse the Olympic Mountains in the distance. Every time she visited Elly it was overcast. Still, Helen thought, the gray day was a nice change from the eternal blue down in San Diego, but for Elly it made dealing with a broken heart that much more sorrowful.

Elly was sitting on the floor, a box of old papers and notebooks in front of her. She looked up as Helen walked in and said, "I never thought something so pathetic would ever happen to me. I mean, I'm in my thirties."

"Pathetic isn't strong enough a word for what that bastard did to you. And what does it matter how old you are? People get hurt at all ages," Helen replied. "Be glad it wasn't more serious. Be glad the relationship ended before he really hurt you."

"You don't think being thrown out of a car and cracking my chin open on the pavement is really hurting me, Mom?"

"I didn't mean that, Elly. Of course he really hurt you.

What he did to you was horrible," Helen said, noticing the small scab on her daughter's chin. "Maybe we should sic your father on him."

Elly leaned back against the wall. "You didn't tell Daddy?" she asked.

"No. Did you want me to? I thought if you wanted him to know, you'd tell him yourself," Helen said. Even if it made her feel a touch guilty, Helen was glad that Elly hadn't told Jerry, that she was the parent who got called in case of emergency. Helen loved that she and Elly could be so open with each other. Most of her friends complained about not having an intimate enough relationship with their kids, but Helen and Elly could be honest, sometimes even brutally so. "Honey, I know this is tough for you," she said, "but what's hurting you more? The cut on your chin or that he's never going to call you again?"

Elly put her hand dramatically to her chest. "Youch," she said. She rubbed her face, her small hands barely covering her features. "I haven't told you, but I wrote him a letter." Elly looked down at the floor and shook her head to herself. "I apologized to him for making him mad."

Helen looked at Elly.

"I'm an idiot. Shit. That was last week. Now, of course, I can't believe I did it, but I can't take it back."

"Did he write back?" Helen asked. The sun began to peer out behind gray wisps of clouds. She turned her head and searched the horizon for white-domed mountains, but they were still obscured by a distant retreating storm.

"No. I don't expect him to." Her mouth formed a pout. "I'm so humiliated by this." She looked away from Helen's gaze toward the pile of loose-leaf paper and notebooks on the floor in front of her outstretched legs.

Time to move on, Helen gathered from Elly's silence. "What on earth are you doing down there on the floor? What are all those papers?" Helen asked.

"This is my diary from when we first moved to California." Elly showed her a small pink diary with an aged golden lock attached to the cover. "I was looking through it this morning. Reading about my adolescence. I was always so crazy about boys. So many boys. Butch, Danny, Tommy. Here we were, moving back and forth across the country and so much of my life revolved around getting boys to like me." She laughed. "Not that I've changed a whole hell of a lot."

Helen leaned forward and fluffed her hair in the back. "Your grandfather would have called you a *tsatskele*."

"Is that Hebrew? What's it mean?"

"No, it's Yiddish. I always thought it meant a loose girl," Helen replied. "Whenever we'd pass a couple necking, he'd shake his head and mutter, '*tsatskele*.' I'd laugh when he said it, even if I got slapped for it."

"That's a pretty word. It's a wonder Yiddish isn't

offered as a second language in high school." Elly stood up. "I'm going to make some tea. Here. Read this entry," she said, handing Helen the pink book. "The one where we've just moved from Connecticut. What were you thinking, Mom?"

September 5, 1974

Dear Diary,

In California now, dear Diary. And I'm in high school for the first time. It sure is a lot different from Connecticut. On my first day of school Mom dressed me in green slacks and a flowered shirt and penny loafers. I went to the bus stop and talked to a really cute guy named Doug. He lives down the street from us. He was wearing shorts and a T-shirt and flip-flops. I was pretty embarrassed because I looked so damn normal. We stopped at bus stops all along the beach, and each time we did, more and more blonde-haired girls wearing bathing suit tops and skimpy skirts got on. They gave me mostly dirty looks, I guess because I'm new, except from Doug, who kept talking to me. He's a hot surfer and a real popular guy, so I'll just stay by him.

We got to school and Doug asked me if I wanted to smoke a cig and I said sure. We went up to the old baseball field behind the school. There were lots of people smoking cigarettes. I made a bunch of friends besides Doug, like another new girl, Brenda. She's from Mississippi. That was fun writing that. Mississippi. The song is in my head at the same time I'm writing it.

"I remember that girl Brenda. Didn't her mother have lung cancer?" Helen yelled toward the kitchen, where she heard Elly squeezing the honey bear, little gasps of air coming between globs. And Helen remembered too that feeling of newness, of insecurity, of the certainty no one would accept her. Only it wasn't from high school that she so vividly remembered that fear of rejection. It was when she was in the presence of her new mother-in-law, Esther.

"You're too young to get married, Jerry," she had harped over and over, often in front of Helen herself. She didn't care who knew her feelings. Her firstborn should get a decent job, make a living for a while before taking such a big step. But they married anyway, and even at the wedding, Helen in her mother's refurbished gown and Jerry in a rented black tux, tall and mature, Esther showed the couple no joy. It was as if the ceremony were for someone else's child and she was the cleaning woman waiting for it to end so she could go home and rest her feet.

When Helen got pregnant four months later, the scolding started all over again. "A man your age doesn't need to be weighed down by a baby. Do you have any idea how much a baby is going to cost you?" She paced back and forth in front of them. They were living with her then, so there was no escape from her pointed forefinger. And when Helen miscarried, when the blood dripped the life from inside her, Helen understood that Esther had somehow cursed the baby.

"Mom, what did you think? Can you believe I was such a

dweeb?" Elly sat down on the couch next to Helen and handed her a mug of steaming chamomile tea, sweetened just right (of course in her own home she would have used Sweet'N Low, but who's complaining?). "Everything moved so quickly for me then. Sex before I was ready . . . Jesus, what was I? Thirteen?"

"What? What sex? I thought you said your first time was with that boyfriend you had your senior year. Jeremy."

"Yeah, well, I guess at this point you should know the truth. Jeremy wasn't my first. He was like my third or so. Sorry, Mom. You want to read about it, or should I tell you?"

Helen grabbed for the diary. No, this was not a story to be shared out loud, like the bedtime stories of Elly's childhood: *Goodnight Moon*, *Green Eggs and Ham*, and of course, *The Lorax*—all those Truffula Trees!—her favorite. Helen recalled her daunting child, Elly, volunteering with all those anti-nuke or Save the Whale groups where she always managed to sneak into her newsletters and speeches the plight of the endangered Truffula. Now look at her: her only cause these days is trying to grow into womanhood.

November 14, 1974

Dear Diary,

I'm in trouble now. All sorts with the folks. Last weekend I told them I was going to Nancy's house but what really happened was Nancy and me and Thea went to a party at a vacant apartment where Joel

*and his brother live. We drank lots of beer and then Joel and Thea
started having SEX right there in front of everybody and then Marco,
this cute surfer dude who I really liked, and Kyle started kissing me
together and then they took my pants off and Kyle sort of held me down
and Marco did it to me. I felt so stupid while it was happening because
I didn't know what I was doing and I lost my retainer somewhere and
I cried a little too. Then Kyle took me home and said he was sorry
about what happened and I said it was okay, it didn't hurt and I
was glad I wasn't a virgin anymore since I was the only girl I knew
who was.*

*When I got home my mom and dad were waiting up for me and
they were sooooo mad because after I left, Nancy's mom called about
something and they said I was supposed to be there with Nancy but she
said no, Nancy was supposed to be at MY house. They were yelling at
me and there I was sitting in that white chair in their bedroom with
my underwear stuffed in my coat pocket and I could feel blood or
something making me all wet. They grounded me for a month, but I
know they'll change their minds.*

I hope I don't get preggers.

"Oh, God. I remember that night," Helen said. "I remember thinking that it was good that your father finally had
the guts to punish you for something. I'm so sorry that happened. How awful. Why didn't you tell me then?"

"Please. I am so over it. I didn't tell you then because

we weren't exactly the best of friends. I was too busy lying to
you and running around with as many bad boys as I could
find. Maybe some therapist would tell me it's the unconscious
reason for my desperate behavior with men, but no, I feel no
pain about it now." Elly took a sip of her tea. "What did you
mean about being glad Dad was mad at me?"

"From the moment you were born, you became the
center of his universe. You were truly the light in his eyes."
Helen got up and lowered the shade behind her partway. "You
don't mind? The glare is giving me a headache.

"He used to take you out for breakfast, just the two of
you. You remember that?" Helen asked.

"Sure I do." Elly sat stiffly, cross-legged, wrapping and
unwrapping her shoelace around her finger. "He'd sneak in
and 'ssshhh' me with his finger to his mouth. Then we'd go
to The Pancake House. Was that a big deal? Me eating chocolate chip pancakes with him and not everyone else?"

Helen smiled. She had sometimes been jealous of their
intimate time together. But it was Elly's older brother, Brian,
who'd really taken it hard. He'd wanted his father's love so
much; it was torture watching him try to squeeze even the ti-
niest bit from that man, like trying to squeeze juice from a
month-old lemon.

"He loved you. But he should have tried to hand out
his love a little more evenly, that's all I'm saying." Helen

started flipping through the pages of Elly's pink-striped book, smeared with ancient and permanent fingerprints. "What an awful experience to have for your first time with sex."

"Not as bad as the first time I got drunk. Remember me throwing up on you, and you and Dad dragging me out of the house all day as punishment?" Elly took the diary from Helen. "Here, listen to this. 'February 12, 1975. Dear Diary, Ugh! I hate this place. I hate my parents too. They are so mean to me, not letting me go out with boys or anything. They're mad because my grades are bad, but school is so stupid. The teachers are all idiots.

" 'My new best friend is Donna. She just moved here from Chicago and I made friends with her so she'd feel good like people did for me when I was new. We take walks and go to the Thrifty drugstore and hang out and eat ice-cream cones. I wish I was still in Connecticut, though, because people don't really like me as much as I want them to.

" 'I was Glenn's girlfriend last week, but he stopped calling me after we went to a party at Don's together, maybe because I drank so much of that drink V.O. and cranberry juice Don gave me. I sure was sick from drinking that. And my parents got so mad again just because I was drunk.

" 'I got home and tried to sleep, but the room was spinning and spinning, my walls were doing cartwheels without me and so I called MOM MOM! and she came into my room and I told her maybe I drank too much at that party and she was mad but also nice and took me into the bathroom and made me drink Alka-Seltzer, which made me throw up and feel a little better. BUT! the next day both Mom and Dad came into my room real early and said, "Rise and shine. Today is the day we're going to Universal Studio Tours," and I said no way since I felt like crap. But they dragged me out of bed and I sat in the car between my brothers for the two-hour ride to Los Angeles and had to go on all the tours, with my head still feeling crappy and foggy and my stomach turning somersaults. We took a tram that ran over a collapsing bridge that made my head feel like it would collapse too. And we sat in some stupid made-up studio audience and pretended we were watching the filming of some movie, even though I knew it wasn't the real thing. The worst part was when the tram stopped at the Parting of the Red Sea from *The Ten Commandments,* which made me dizzy with all that water going over and around us like chaos and I begged my dad to get me a Coke or something.

"'I'm not going to drink ever again, that's for sure. Maybe that's what their plan was, and if it was, well, it worked.'"

"You see, I was smarter than you thought. Sorry you hated me so much," Helen said.

"You were smart about Butch, that's for sure. He stole that ring, that opal one, you know, for me." Elly knelt back down over her papers. "It only took me two years to get up the nerve to break up with him. I knew he was bad blood, but he was my beloved Butch. Here's the letter he wrote me after he got mine." She showed Helen the crumpled, then flattened, yellow-lined paper. "It never sunk in that I was breaking up with him. He wrote this from juvenile hall. 'Elly,' " she read. " 'I got your letter today and read it and am really pissed. You are holding a lot of shit against me when you don't even give me a chance to explain myself to you. You should be writing to me giving me encouragement instead of putting me down as low as you can. And you should be telling me you love me instead of saying your love for me flew right out the window. I mean your love for me shouldn't die like that. If you love me like you said you did, then you would stick by me through thick and thin. Yeah, I promised you I would stay straight, but you have to understand that I enjoy getting high and being bad once in a while. But you should love me for what I am and stand by me. And about that robbery bullshit, you should know I have a bad record around where I live and all the cops know me. Now they're trying to nail me for something I didn't do. That's why I'm fighting back in court this time. But even my parents want me to do time until I'm eighteen. And I know I couldn't handle doing time again, especially for something I didn't do. So my lawyer is trying to get me into a group home. I still plan on being with you in time and being with you forever.

    " 'Well, it is the next morning now and I am feeling a lot better. I love you, babe, and wish I could see you. Keep that promise that you will love me forever and that will be enough to keep me straight in here. Because my love for you will never die. Just keep writing to me and giving me your support, babe, because I just don't want to receive letters like the one you just sent me. I can't handle it. You won't have to try and change me back to the guy you fell in love with, because I haven't changed any since I saw you last, except a lot better. I want to love you and love you forever. Well, babe, I guess I'd better be going now. I really hope you understand. Take extra special care of yourself, for me. And babe, don't forget, write me back and make it long. Love ya much and always will. Love, Butch.' "

Helen sighed. "He was not my favorite, that Butch, but I remember how much you thought you loved him."

"You remember that?" Elly asked.

"Sweetheart. You're my child. How could I forget the way your face lit up whenever you got one of those letters, or when he called you? Speaking of calling, I want to check my messages."

"Mom. Hello! You've only been gone a couple of hours. Who are you expecting to call? That Paul guy? The golfer?"

"As a matter of fact . . ."

"But you hate golf."

"Yes, but he's very handsome and is quite taken with the fact that I live on a golf course. He thinks as long as I do, I should learn how to play."

Helen got up from the couch and stretched her arms above her head, then reached them down and bounced, attempting to touch the floor. Her back was not so good these days. As a matter of fact, her whole body was in a bit of a bind. If she was going to have sex with someone other than Jerry for the first time, she'd need to start toning her lazy muscles.

"Do you miss Dad?"

"What?" Helen hadn't expected that question, and now the few loose muscles in her body went taut.

"Do you mean do I miss going out to a restaurant and not having to put in an extra dollar because I ordered a side of avocado?"

"No, seriously."

"I'm being serious." Helen started walking toward the kitchen phone. She stopped and looked back at Elly's upturned face. "I miss going out with a man on Saturday nights. I miss feeling safe in his arms. I miss the feel of a man's breath on my back as I fall asleep. I miss having a companion." She walked into the kitchen.

But I don't miss his snoring or his change of moods, or the way he read the paper at the dinner table when I yearned to talk to someone, to tell someone about my day. Helen dialed her number in San Diego.

"Your brother called," Helen said, walking back into the room. "He and Maggie are fighting again. Talking about going back to court. He's going to be the death of me."

Elly looked at the floor. "You don't think maybe he was part of the death of your and Dad's marriage in the first place?"

Helen didn't want to lie to Elly; she no longer had reason to hide the losses that Brian's breakdown had caused. The marriage was over. "Yes. I do. But only partly. No one in particular is to blame for the divorce. Can we get back to talking about you?"

"I'm sorry for bringing it up," Elly said. "I just thought maybe as long as you're here and if you wanted to talk about it. I mean, it's not like we all got together and discussed the divorce."

Helen sat down on the couch. Actually, it did feel good to talk about her life. It was like the unclogging of a stuck drain. "And what, so I should feel guilty that your father didn't consult the three of you before falling in love with another woman?" She waved her hand in the air in front of her. She hated Jerry for humiliating her by leaving first. Once, many years ago, when the kids were small, Helen had awakened one morning and felt as if she no longer loved Jerry, wondered if she had rushed into the marriage too quickly, mistaken security for romance. At breakfast, after the children had gone off to school, she'd asked him to lower the newspaper he was reading.

"Jerry," she'd started slowly. "Jerry. I think maybe I don't love you as much as I'm supposed to."

"What the hell does that mean, Helen?" he'd asked, more anger than hurt in his voice.

She had no idea what it meant, but she knew he was waiting for an answer. "It means that maybe we should think about separating," she said, but really she had no interest in a life without him in it. She didn't want to be a divorcée, didn't want to open up alimony checks every month, didn't want to date her hairdresser's brother. She just wanted her husband to know that she wasn't in love with him.

Her response seemed to kick open something inside him. He had taken her hand tightly in his and told her, "I love you, Helen. I won't be able to live without you. Don't ever leave me."

That was the only time, as far as Helen knew, that Jerry had begged for anything. His own mother had given him everything, pampering him long enough to ensure he would take care of her when she needed him to. Helen had agreed not to leave him that day, of course, and every day the marriage edged a bit closer to something more comfortable than ever before. But a cold stillness remained between them, like fog on a mountain lake at sunrise.

"What happened with me and your father started long before Brian's illness," Helen said, her right palm cupping her chin, her fingers feeling the smoothness of her right cheek. "Elly. Your dad and I didn't love each other enough."

"Then why'd you stay together so long?" Elly asked, standing up and going into her bedroom. She came back wearing a Brown University sweatshirt. She sat down next to Helen and looked at her, awaiting her answer.

Helen let her eyes drift around the small room. The dimming light behind her moved shadows across Elly's seashell collection perched atop a small shelf running the length of the back wall. She imagined for a moment that she could hear the sounds of the waves coming from the tiny openings. Do you tell your own child that the reason you stayed in a loveless marriage is because you'd wanted to give her and her brothers stability?

"I'm not sure," was all she said.

"Was it because there was nothing better out there for you?" Elly pushed.

"Better? I don't know, Elly. You know how your grandfather treated me. You know I needed to get away from him. Your father came along and got me out of that house. If it hadn't been him, it would have been the next guy."

Elly stared at her.

"Does that really shock you?" Helen asked.

"A little. Yeah. But from a totally selfish standpoint. I want to believe true love exists, Mom. I wanted to have my parents be madly in love with each other. I want to be madly in love," Elly said.

Helen saw tears forming in Elly's eyes. She rose from the couch and pulled Elly up with her. "Come here, baby."

She drew Elly tightly into her arms and rocked her back and forth, remembering distinctly how Elly smelled as a baby. Helen sighed and breathed in her daughter's scent again and again.

That night Elly let Helen take her diary to bed with her. Waves of guilt and regret flowed over her as she read of her daughter's adolescent meanderings, daily dramas, and angst-stained words. How could she and Jerry not have been more aware of the pain their transitions caused the children?

January 14, 1976

Dear Diary,

I hate it here. I can't believe we moved back to Connecticut. Nothing is the same and I thought it would be. My old friends, the ones I grew up with since I was a kid, Rachel and Kara and Jody, are all so different now. You'd think I'd been gone a hundred years instead of just one and a half. My new friend Patty and I spend a lot of time at her house listening to music, mostly Jackson Browne. My grades are great even with all this commotion going on. Brian tried to kill himself and I came home to find him asleep on my bed and there was poop all over the bathroom floor. I made him get into his own bed. He was soaked with sweat. Yucko, all around. My folks came home and found out he took all of Mom's Valium but he didn't die. Mom and Dad are trying to

figure him out and that's been pretty tough on them, it's obvious. Dad's
coming home less and less for dinner and Mom's smoking like a chimney.
Evan is being ignored, poor thing. Why is Brian so depressed? I'd ask
him, but I'm too busy hating him for what he's doing to the family.

The image of her son sweating in his bed, waiting for the
ambulance to arrive, wandered unhurriedly across Helen's
mind. Jerry tried to ignore the neighbors' looks as the ambulance came for him that night. He got good at ignoring looks
from other people.

Helen closed the pink book and reached over to the
chair to grab her bathrobe, using it to cover her chilled feet.
She breathed in the smell of the rain in the night air hovering
over Puget Sound.

Brian's depression had gotten worse, and they'd committed him to an institution where the treatment had worked,
for the most part. He'd mellowed with medication and therapy,
and eventually married Maggie, though they are now divorced
and sharing custody of their daughter, Samantha. Helen has
faith that little Samantha will continue to give her oldest son
enough of a reason to wake up and smile every day. For Helen,
her three children are the best reasons to wake to the sun
filtering through her Venetian blinds every San Diego morning. What else is there now but her children, Helen thinks as
she pushes the propped-up pillow down to the bed, punching
a hole in the middle so her hair will not flatten so much.

Prairie Dogs

We weren't starving. But still. My sister and brother took whatever work the town would dole out to them. Sissy washed floors after school at the Good Neighbors Nursing Home and Doon worked the orchards when the season allowed. Mama worked her tiny brown-speckled hands turning rags and yarn and thread into quilts and sweaters. She sold whatever she could to the summer strangers who came to the weekend arts and crafts fairs, hoping to find some real steals.

I used to peddle my paintings there. Mama said my pictures were real good and my God-blessed hands shouldn't touch nothing but fine brushes and smooth canvas. I had learned a little about colors and paints when I took the Beginning Art course at the college. Mama and Aunt Wanda paid for it from the money Doon gave them out of the goodness of his heart every month. Out of the goodness of his heart, and fear that he was not too old to get a good walloping from Mama.

I sold my paintings as quickly as I painted them, two or three every summer weekend, making at least two hundred dollars. It wasn't a lot, but it saved me from serving up vanilla soft serves at the Dairy Freeze. Then that tall stranger found me.

It was another sunny Sunday, the kind that makes me want to take Doon's truck and drive into the hills so as to take the colors of the earth back home with me. I unfold my easel as my eyes wander over the red dirt, the blue sky lying hard across the rough ridges. Then what I do next, I close my eyes, breathe deeply through my nose, out through my mouth five times. Not four. Not six. I read in some old yoga magazine I found in the thrift store that five times is all it takes to relax the mind and all. With my brain all loosened up and my eyes closed, I fix on one image, something I stir up using my imagination. I might see a horse galloping on only its hind legs with a red jester's hat on, or maybe a herd of fat cows having a tea party under the shade of a juniper. I open my eyes and look at a real-world place right in front of me. I mix it all together like Mama does when she's making corn pudding in a bowl. This is the picture I paint. Some of what I see, some of what I breathe in.

The man in the stiff jeans and orange snakeskin boots

stopped in front of our stand, stared at one of my paintings—
the one with our dog Pablo on the back of a big bull riding
across the burnt brown and red-streaked mesa into the dripping violet sunset—and asked me my name. But first he looked
me up and down like I was a dirty whore and he was low on
money.

"Lydia. Why?"

"I like your paintings. A lot," he said, his eyes now easing a
bit into friendliness. "There are some other people, friends
of mine who've seen these and think you've got some talent."

"What do you mean, *some* talent?" Mama struck back
from her lounge chair. "Lydia's going to be famous."

"Well, madam, I agree, and that's why I'm here to talk
about a painting job for Miss Lydia."

The man starts talking to me about a business propo-
sition, and Mama leans over past her cardboard *Handmade From
the Heart* sign and tries to warn that man away with her blue
knitting needle that Grandma Mavis gave her. But I tell her,
"Shh, Mama. Let me listen to what this gentleman is offering."

And this man talks some, and I listen with Mama
breathing so heavy beside me, I think maybe she's sick, or the
sun is getting to her, and finally the man in the orange boots
leaves.

Maybe he thought I'd throw myself at those dead snake
feet of his, thanking him for the offer to paint a wall of the

baby nursery for those people up at that Wild Rose Ranch. The ones we here in town hear about from time to time. I pretended I didn't know anything at all about those rich folks, but to tell the truth, I got hooked on those people the day the local news reported they were moving in.

It was about two years ago, and I was helping Sissy with her cleaning at Good Neighbors. Okay, so I wasn't really cleaning, just hanging out with Charlotte Hernandez. She and Mama were schoolgirls together way back. A few years ago Charlotte fell and broke her hip, and since there was no family near to help her while she was healing, she got put up in the home. Mama thanked God every day for her own three angels, who "would sooner let the devil in for breakfast than send their mama to the old folks' home."

Nobody much cared to visit Charlotte, including Mama, who thought it might bring her bad luck if she stepped foot inside that place, so I tagged along with Sissy a couple of times a month just to sit with Charlotte.

There was this one day when Charlotte just slept the whole time I was there, so I distracted myself for a few hours reading the newspaper and magazines, a habit I picked up when I was a pinprick of a girl. I read just about anything I could get my eyes and hands on. Reading was my best friend, and I cheated on her only with my true love, painting.

The paper made some big stink that day about the

Fancy Folks—the senator from Virginia and his beautiful actress wife—who'd bought a huge cattle ranch outside town past the National Monument.

I used to look every day for word about them. Mama and the rest couldn't care less about them or the goings-on up at that ranch, but Sally Escobar and Valerie Gasper got hooked right away too, and we did some detective work at the feed and grain supply store. We talked to Ralph at the accounting desk—seeing how he's Sally's stepbrother—and got the lowdown on the names of some of the hired ranch hands and when it was they usually came to town for supplies.

We waited like dumb girls one morning, and when Jesus and Chuck showed up in a Wild Rose Ranch truck, we just went crazy giggling and flirting till we got them to go have a root beer float with us down at Dotty's.

They said the senator never spent much time at the ranch. They had never seen the movie star, but Chuck said he'd give his right arm to. They said the senator built himself and his wife a fine house tucked into some tall piñon pines. There was a lap pool, and four lazy Maine coon cats that hung around inside all day just licking themselves.

The senator ran a herd of Brahman. Strange-looking creatures, Brahmans. They aren't as ugly as the lumpy, cream-colored Charolais, not as handsome as the fat-boy Herefords. With their floppy ears, dog faces, and great horned backs, they make that Quasimodo hunchback seem kind of cute. I like to

paint cows, especially Angus, with their wavering eyelashes falling off those dark brown eyes, like they have no business hanging there in the first place. When I'm coming up with a
picture, I laugh out loud just thinking about cows or dogs
looking all well-mannered out there on that great high desert.
Cows and dogs and even jackrabbits look silly when I paint
them playing and prancing around against God's finest work.
I like to think those nutty animal adventures make folks smile
some. And buy my paintings, of course.

Here I was thinking I knew the ins and outs of that
Wild Rose Ranch and that it wasn't all that exciting when put
all together on one plate, when out of nowhere that tall man
comes over and offers me a whopping fifteen hundred dollars
just to paint a wall. Mister Orange Boots told me the senator
had seen my paintings one Saturday when he was in town and
really liked them, especially the cow pictures. Jeez. My pictures
on a rich baby's wall. Now, that was nothing like having the
devil over for pancakes!

The plan was that I would meet the ranch hands,
George and Rudy, at the feed store Monday morning with my
painting gear and they would drive me back to the ranch. He
said the ranch manager, Wade Marshall, would be there to
meet me and show me the wall and everything. I didn't sleep
too well that long night, with so much to think about. I tossed
around quietly so as not to wake Sissy, smiling and snoring
under the brown and gold crocheted blanket Mama made for

her. For a while I looked past the old red-checkered curtain billowing in from the wind and counted the stars splashed against the sky, so narrow and dark. I thought about getting up and sketching the stars down onto a white sky, like turning the world inside out, but I just listened to my heart beat quick and steady instead.

Mama made me a lunch of bologna and cheese sandwiches. I showed up an hour early at the supply store and just browsed around, touching my fingertips to the dusty shelves and kicking the bags of feed. When the truck skidded roughly over the gravel in the parking lot, my ears must have perked up higher than the top of my black-haired head and my heart snuck up to my dry throat. I grabbed my stuff and ran out to meet my ride out of town.

"You the painter girl?" asked the blond boy.

"I am. I sure appreciate the ride," I replied quietly.

They told me I could wait in the Ford while they loaded up some salt blocks. I climbed in and immediately gagged from the smell of that closed-in space filled with the stench of sweat and rust and old meat. The boys got in and the smell got a whole lot worse, but I was still glad to be going. I breathed through my mouth and looked out the window the whole two-hour ride out to the ranch.

The house they dropped me in front of was a lot smaller than what I expected. It was a log house in the middle of an immense valley floor. A clump of cedar trees loomed over the rooftop and sheltered the small green lawn. I looked all around me in a circle and took in the high red hills completely surrounding the spread. The screen door slammed, I looked up, and Wade Marshall walked the five steps it took to find my hand with his.

Now, let the record show that I'd had a boyfriend or two in my short lifetime. I preferred painting to kissing, but now and then I'd tag along to the movies with Valerie and her gang of friends from the mill. There was this one fellow, Dusty Begay, who had long black hair that I loved to tug whenever he tried to snuggle me in the backseat of his Chevy. Tugging hair is one thing. Setting eyes on a stranger and feeling your hands get all sweaty inside of four seconds is quite another.

That Wade Marshall was the most beautiful man I'd ever set my eyes on. He was a vision I didn't need any imagination to make more perfect. Wearing a black Stetson and scuffed cowboy boots under blue jeans that fit his leg muscles like they were painted there, he leaned forward and took my hand before I had the chance to swat the sweat off it.

"Hi, Lydia, I'm Wade. It's good of you to come all this way. Where's the rest of your stuff?" His blue eyes sparkled like moonlight sprayed across a glacial lake.

"Right here," I said, picking up my pack. "I got what I need here to get the picture sketched and started at least."

"No, I mean your clothes and such. Didn't Mac tell you you'd be living up here for a spell?"

"No, he didn't," I said, now flustered enough to let my pack slip back down to the ground.

"Damn that Mac. Another no-good bureaucrat playing smarter than he is. You have any problem moving into the house for a couple weeks while you do the mural? It's a heck of a trip down to town, and the boys are too busy now."

"Uh-huh," was all I could muster. These were a lot of thoughts for my head. My insides felt like one of my tubes of paints must feel with me squeezing it all day long.

"How long you reckon it'll take?" He was polite, not pushy. I told him I needed to see the wall and I could take a guess. I confessed that I'd never painted anything bigger than what I could tuck under my arm. He led me in.

The inside of the house was the coziest place I'd ever set foot. There were elk and deer hides covering the furniture, and antlers were made into hanging hooks just about everywhere you looked. The floor was beat-up hardwood covered here and there with brightly-colored rugs that looked like they belonged on the ground in someone's tipi. There was a filled-to-the-brim bookshelf against a wall and a big leather chair set up next to it just waiting for someone to flop down and spend a whole month flipping pages. I didn't see any cats around, but I heard a dog barking outside the four-paned window facing east toward the darkening sky.

I almost wished aloud how my heart was wanting more

than anything to live here and be Wade's wife, but I was business-like when he walked me into the baby's room and pointed at the wall. It was about eight feet high and ten feet wide.

There were just the four walls, one with a small window peeking out from behind yellow ruffled curtains moving slightly in the breeze. A lone cot covered with a storybook quilt took up some empty space in the middle of the wood floor.

"I suppose it'll take me some weeks to paint this wall. First I have to come up with the picture in my head, you see, then I need to sketch it out and—"

"A week or two is what we were expecting," Wade interrupted. I was glad he did, or I probably would've gone on to tell him my horoscope sign or something equally as stupid as that. I was brain stuck around him, that's all there was to it, but I knew what I was here to do, so I took a deep breath. "Fine," I said. "Would it be okay if I phoned my mama to tell her about staying out here?"

"No problem," Wade said.

I hesitated, then added, "Could someone maybe drive me to my house tomorrow to fetch some of my clothes and buy the art supplies?" I was already imagining Mama's nervous hands twisting around each other in suspicion while she watched me pack.

"I suppose I got no problem with that. It was damn stupid of me to think that Mac could have got it right," he said, sighing and rubbing his perfect face. "I'll set it up. I hope you can see fit to staying tonight with nothing but what you got."

"I got no problem with that," I said, hoping he'd smile at my mock. He did and I started to relax.

"Do you mind sleeping on the couch out in the den?" Wade asked.

"Not a bit," I said. "It'll keep me close to my work." I stared at the white wall for a beat, then looked at Wade. I set my things down and took a new look around the room. The quilt had a brown teddy bear wearing a red ribbon and reading a nursery rhyme book to his teddy friends. I knew I was going to have some fun for the next two weeks.

"This baby's one lucky angel. Is it the senator's?"

Wade's shoulders stiffened and a grimace crossed his mouth; his face frowned and smiled all in one go. I thought for a second he was either going to cry or punch the wall.

"I guess you could say that," he said, and walked out the door mumbling something about talking to Rudy. I grabbed my sketchbook and wandered into the kitchen to phone Mama and make the acquaintance of the ranch cook, Rosa, who was chopping up onions and tomatoes for salsa. After the fifteen minutes it took to calm Mama down, I sat at the table and listened to Rosa hum a song as the dark smells of the chili she was cooking filled my nose. We smiled at each other now and then, but she was happy to let me sit there and draw, and I felt fine about leaving her to her habañeros.

Wade showed up a while later and Rosa served us dinner. She didn't eat with us. She waited for us to finish and then went to her cabin in the workers' camp. It was just Wade and me at the table, and I thought for sure I'd be too nervous to eat, like maybe I'd miss my mouth with the spoon or something just as clumsy. Wade read a cattle magazine while he ate and I watched him when I knew he didn't know it. He just gulped his food down and drank a huge glass of milk. Ignoring his napkin, he wiped his mouth with a white cloth he took from his pants pocket and left the table. Just as he reached the door, I remembered to ask him, "Wade, I heard you had a lap pool here."

"What? That's up at the senator's house." He opened the door. "Good night," he said, as he walked out into the kind of moonlight no lovers should be kept from. "See you tomorrow."

The door closed. I figured then it would be best to mind my own business, paint the picture, get my money, and go on home.

That night I dreamt of bright yellow caterpillars turning into newborn babies with wings.

The next morning Wade gave me two hundred dollars and told me to buy whatever I needed. He said it was extra to the fifteen hundred dollars I'd get when the mural was done. Rudy and I drove the long drive into town with his radio playing loud rock and roll all the way. Rudy must have showered that morning, because I didn't have to hold my breath at all this time. I told him where to drop me. I hugged Mama hello, packed my stuff, then took Doon's truck and got what paints and all I needed. Turned out to cost little more than half what I had in my front pocket. So I took Mama and Sissy out for a lunch at the Blue Moon Tavern. Mama felt better about me being gone for some ten days after she got her sweaty iced-tea glass refilled five times. Mama loves a free refill.

After we got back, Rudy drove me around the ranch so I could get my fill of Brahman cows. I had a gut feeling that I had to have them in the mural. I watched them as close up as I could, while Rudy filled the salt licks. I wanted to know what they were thinking, what to have them doing. That's the breathing part of my painting: what I watch and what I think of while I'm breathing with my eyes closed have got to do a tango together, put their arms around each other and pull in tight, face-to-face.

I used some of the nature books I found on the bookshelves in the den to see what other animals I wanted to have playing around with the cows. I got details on the white-tailed prairie dog with his fur all yellow-streaked, and that cute black spot over his eye. Their bird playmate was going to be a chukar, just about the prettiest bird hiding in the rocks around here.

Finally, on Wednesday morning after a nice bowl of oatmeal and some venison sausage on the side, I went outside, sat under a tree, did my breathing exercises, and found the picture in my head. I made the sketch with my Prismacolor pencils: the setting was the towering red rock mesas and sage plains in the background, and aspen trees all around the sides. Rudy drove me through a stand of those graceful quaking aspens, and I knew they were the proper kind of tree for a baby's room, so upright and thin like ballerinas. On the left side of the picture there'd be a big Brahman scratching his hide against the white bark of a tree and some of the small round green leaves would be fluttering down to the ground. Right above the middle, riding on a leaf like it was a magic carpet, a red-beaked chukar with its blindfold of black around its eyes would float down. Another partridge and his prairie dog friend on the ground would be looking up at him as if to say, "Buddy, what are you doing flying around up there on that leaf?" And off to the right side, two big-humped cows with their flabby dewlaps would be watching the scene and smiling, while underneath them, camped out in the shade of their enormous bellies, three yellow prairie dogs would be playing jacks. Soft yellows and greens mostly, set off by some strong reds and blacks. I liked it and decided it was best to forget all about that Wade and set to painting it.

The work went easy. I'd wake in the mornings whenever I heard Rosa out in the kitchen making coffee. Wade and I would sometimes eat together in the sunny corner, him reading one of his magazines, me sketching on a pad and humming quietly to myself. He'd ask me how it's going, then get up before I could even answer him. I'd clear my dishes, thank Rosa, and go to the nursery. I ate lunch alone. Dinners were pretty much the same as breakfast. A nod hello. Then Wade would get up after eating and head outside to smoke or take a walk with his dog, Jack.

I went to town with Rudy on Sunday so he could go to church and I could pick up more paints, and visit Mama and them. When we got back to the ranch midday, there was a green car parked next to the small wooden shack by the house. I walked inside and saw Wade hugging a tall skinny guy.

"Lydia, this here's my kid brother, Robert, all the way from college in California. He and his friend are going to be staying on a few weeks. If they get in your way," he grinned, "you just let me know and I'll shoot 'em."

"Hi, Lydia. I'm Elly," the girl coming into the room said. She was pretty, lanky like her boyfriend. Maybe a year or two older than I was, nineteen or twenty. "I hope you don't mind, but I just checked out your mural. It's really amazing."

During dinner that night Wade and Robert joked non-stop. As the brothers hugged good night, Elly moved to look directly into Wade's eyes and said, "See you in the morning, Wade."

Robert and Elly slept in the little wooden bunkhouse next door. On their first morning they slept through breakfast. Wade went outside afterward and fired a shotgun right by their window. Robert came dashing out with only his boxers on. "You bastard," he yelled as he ran after Wade, both of them laughing.

When the next morning's eggs and fried elk steaks were all but cold, Wade grabbed a bow and arrow off the den wall. I followed him outside and held my hand to my mouth to quiet my giggles as he drew back and let an arrow—THWOOOOP!— hit the side of their quarters. First one. Then another arrow. After three loud thumps of metal hitting wood, Robert stumbled out the door. "Yeah. Yeah," he said, zipping up his blue jeans. "You're so goddamn macho. Say, Sitting Bull, why don't you go rustle this cowboy up some decent grub."

"I'm on my way to deal with the fields. You can grab lunch later. You're the one who whined about wanting to learn how to work a ranch. We're leaving now," he said, so seriously, even the sight of those arrows stuck there in the wood didn't seem so funny anymore. Robert grabbed a shirt and jumped in the truck. They drove off together.

Elly came into the nursery a little while later.

"You didn't get woken up by those arrows?" I asked in disbelief.

"Sure I did. I just didn't want Wade to see me all puffy and sleepy-eyed."

I didn't quite know what to say, so I just went back to painting my little prairie-dog face.

"He's so beautiful, I almost can't breathe when I'm around him, you know?" she revealed out loud. "I mean, I know you couldn't care less, but I'm not *with* Robert. We're not boyfriend and girlfriend, even though he thought bringing me here would change that."

"Uh-huh. He seems nice," was all I could gather up. I got the feeling I was getting invited to a party I wasn't sure I wanted to attend.

"Oh, he is," she said, trying to convince me she had some grace. "I met him at one of my parties about six months ago. He came up and introduced himself and we talked for about thirty seconds. Then I went off to get another beer and I never saw him again.

"Months go by and five days ago I get a call from him. 'I'm going to work on my brother's ranch. Do you want to come with me?' he says."

She walked over to the wall and traced the outline of one of my trees with her finger. "I had nothing else to do this summer. I could've taken some classes or worked, but it sounded good, going off with a cute guy who told my friend Sharon that he thought I was beautiful, and here we are. Robert thinks he's in love and all I can think about is his brother." She did some weird neck stretches and went on. I couldn't wait for her to leave so I could get back to the dog.

"I can't believe I'm even saying this out loud," she

whined a little. "I mean, I know he's taken, and by a senator's daughter, no less. I'm such an idiot," she said, scratching at a bug bite on her arm.

I stopped in mid-breath. "He's married? Wade's married?"

"Well, not married. Not yet, anyway. Robert told me that when Julia—she's the senator's daughter—came out for Christmas with her father, she and Wade fell in love. The senator wasn't too pleased, but she's the kind of girl who gets what she wants. Julia got pregnant and the senator got really pissed 'cause I guess he thinks a ranch manager is not good enough for his princess, but Julia said no way is she not going to have the baby, so now her father is arranging for them to make it *acceptable*."

"It's Wade's baby?" I asked, shocked. I never thought, I mean, what was I thinking? He told me the baby belonged to the senator. Of course it was Wade's baby. Why else would Wade be living in this house? I don't know why I couldn't add up two plus two when the arithmetic was right there in front of me.

"Julia got herself knocked up by one hell of a guy," Elly muttered, and sat down on the edge of the tiny bed.

"I can sure agree to that," I spurted out like a rusty faucet that got turned on and stuck. "I don't much like to paint people, but I'd sure like to paint that face of his and hang his portrait right over my bed," I tittered, and then quickly turned back to the wall and my prairie dogs. Darn. I wanted to slap my own cheek for saying such a rash thing to a stranger.

I looked at the mural like I hadn't seen it before. Wade's little boy or girl was going to be growing up under my painting. I felt my head begin to swell. My feelings danced around and I wasn't sure who was leading and who was getting their toes stepped on.

"Always my luck to find the right guy at the wrong time," Elly said, and left the baby's room.

I stood back from the wall and let my flushed face cool. She didn't pay any attention to my babbling, and that was good. No wonder Wade was brooding. His love and their baby were miles away, so many you could hardly count them between thumb and forefinger stretched wide apart across the map in the next room.

Things got uglier than roadkill soon after Elly told me the story. During dinner that night, and the night after that, the boys talked to each other in hushed tones. They talked mostly about work, the fields, the cows. All the joking up and vanished.

"You suppose Luis will have the engine fixed by to-morrow afternoon?" Robert asked Wade.

"Why? You got something else to do?"

Robert looked at Wade as if he'd hit him or something.

"No, man. I just thought if you didn't need me, well. Shit. Never mind."

Maybe Robert was going to see if he and Elly could work things out. She and Robert weren't talking much. I guess he'd got wind of her infatuation and felt a whole lot of loss. He'd brought her out to the country to woo her, but instead she got herself distracted by Wade's eyes. Easy enough to understand.

The worst of it came over breakfast two days later. Elly asked Wade if she could drive around with him to check up on the herd. Robert blushed and said, "Elly, I thought we'd take Jack and hike up that peak at the end of the valley."

Elly just ignored him and waited for Wade's answer. Wade looked at Robert. I looked at my plate of scrambled eggs and hominy. I was outside their triangle, and what I wanted was to finish my mural and head back home, away from the calm cricket-studded nights and the cool evening breezes that whipped up the dust and the leaves and the matter of living ground.

I missed Mama, and Sissy and Doon. I missed my quiet corner of the sunporch, where I stretched my canvas taut over the wood frames, where I brought out my colored tubes and fixed the wild wind onto the clean white beginning.

Wade got up from the table without a word and slammed the door on his way out. Robert looked at Elly.

"What are you thinking? Jesus, Elly."

"What?" she said.

Robert shook his head back and forth a couple of times like he couldn't believe what his own thoughts were saying to him.

I stood up from the table and brought my dish and coffee cup to the sink. I started to walk into the nursery, when Robert blurted out, "You're killing me," then got up and ran toward their cabin next door. Elly just sat there and stared out the window in front of her. I took a quiet step forward, hoping to escape the room, hoping to calm my racing heart.

"Lydia," she said.

I stopped. "Yeah?"

"Please sit here. Talk to me a second, would you?" she asked. She was so polite and needy that I thought it only right to keep the cows and the dogs and the birds waiting a bit longer. I sat down at the round wooden table tucked into the corner. Elly moved her half-eaten dish away from her. There was just empty space between us now.

I didn't much know who she was, or where she came from. I knew she was smart and pretty and lucky too, being able to go to college in California without a scholarship. I also knew that if she'd lived around the corner, we wouldn't have been friends. Girls like her didn't usually ask advice from girls like me.

"How bad is it, do you think?" she asked me while biting the right side of her lower lip with her top teeth.

I had mean thoughts in my head. I wanted to yell at her and tell her to stop throwing her big selfish ego around the house like a burst-open vacuum bag.

I said, "Which part?"

She put her head in her hands and started to whimper a little. I tried to think of what Mama would say to her. "You know," I started, "a girl like you is going to get any guy she wants. I bet Wade is the first guy ever to ignore you."

She lifted her head and squeezed her eyebrows together, staring straight at me. "Yeah. You're right. Not too many guys have said no to me. Damn. I don't know what I'm doing sometimes."

If she was looking to have me disagree with her, she was looking in the wrong direction.

"Robert is so cool too. I mean, he's really gentle and loving. Brilliant. Like, one of the smartest men I've ever known. It's just that Wade. Man . . ."

She sighed so deeply, I felt it pass right through my chest too.

"Yup. That Wade. Kind of guy most girls don't end up with. Not even girls like you," I said.

"Girls like me," she said sadly. "Girls like me don't deserve men like Robert. The nice ones. How come the nice ones want me? How come I don't want the nice boys?"

This was aiming too far out of my hemisphere. Nice boys. Bad boys. I wanted to get back to thinking about cow tails swatting flies.

"You're great, Lydia. Thanks for listening to me. I know what I've got to do." Elly got up and walked out of the kitchen. I had no idea what I did to help, but I liked being thanked all the same.

Robert and Elly didn't show up at the dinner table that night. Wade and I ate together in silence. Rosa made a huge pot of posole, and I thought it'd be nice to bring some over to the cabin, but I was scared of Wade's dark mood and didn't want to add to it. Late that night I heard someone creep into the kitchen and fiddle with the pots and silverware.

I was brightening up the little silver jacks, adjusting shadows and light the next morning, when I heard Robert's voice through the open window. I peeked around the corner to see what I could through the screen door. Robert and Elly stood at the green car. Elly threw her stuffed backpack into the trunk and shut it.

"You won't always feel this way. Stay and let's make something work between us," Robert said, clearly trying hard to soothe the strain in his voice.

"Don't you understand? I'm making a fool out of my-self. I'm making a fool out of you," Elly said with tears on her cheeks.

Elly came to the door as I backed away from it and she called me outside. She hugged me, told me she expected to see my name on a big gallery invitation one day, and asked me to write my address on the matchbook cover she held out to me. I hugged her back, and for a moment I thought I knew her pain. For a moment I wanted her to stay so that we could become friends.

I went back into the baby's room and looked into my mural. I saw the colors dancing across the crimson desert vista and I saw smiling cows. I heard the green car drive down the dusty road toward the iron gates at the entrance to the ranch.

I live in Denver now in a house with Sissy and Mama. Sissy's taking nursing courses at the university and Mama is content to sit in front of the big-screen TV watching talk shows and fretting aloud over all the worries other people have with their wily and ungenerous children.

The local paper had done a big story on me and the mural, and a good many folks decided to have me paint their walls too.

Wade was greatly appreciative of the cows and birds and prairie dogs that I made play across his child's vision. After I left the ranch, I never heard from him again. I prayed for him and Julia to have a healthy baby, and I suppose they did.

I got a letter from Elly a month after she left the ranch. She sent me a copy of the letter Robert had tucked inside her knapsack before she drove off.

Dear Elly,

There are no whys to this. There are no becauses. . . . It just is this way. You upset me, you made me angry, you made me laugh, you made me love you. You sparked my emotions. What more is there between two people?

Please don't worry about right or wrong. Let's just see what the autumn brings.

Love, Robert

I never did find it in me to write her back, and I didn't get another letter from her again. I am assuming Robert did not find his way into Elly's heart that autumn. I could be wrong. Probably not.

I knew back then what it meant to fuse breath with mind, so as to build light and color and life from nothing. And I know now what it means to be gentle with my feelings, so as to build friendships from everything.

Perdition

HELL BEGAN a few weeks before I scattered my grand-father's ashes over the dried-out ground outside Borrego Springs. Until then, everything had pretty much been easy street for me, gone my way. Mostly. I sissy-skipped through college in Berkeley, then powered my way through dental school. It was a long haul, but I finally hung my sign—Dr. Scott Rusk, D.D.S.—under the shake eaves of a small house in the commercial zone in Vista. Vista, because my grandfather, Alan Rusk, Sr., was living out his waning days at Ridgeview Manor a couple of miles up the road. No one else was around to watch him die. Lucky me.

I can't stand runny omelets, I can't stand plaque, and I can't stand the smell of death on a man's breath. But he was my father's father and I owed the old man that, take it or leave it.

My own dad's dying was shit. Out of nowhere. It was

bad enough not having a mom to begin with. Dad pretty much brought me up himself. We lived together, the three of us, in Oceanside, where Dad was a hotshot real estate guy. Grandpa was always there, old, it seemed, waiting to die.

My new wife, Jessica, couldn't have cared less about the move down to Vista. She traveled in the world of textiles, bought and sold, and it didn't matter where she parked her car, because her car was rarely parked. Her company had an office in San Diego, but she was off to Mexico, Italy, India, you name it, most of the time. They sewed, she touched, dabbled, negotiated deals for the big guys, made the designers squeal.

I scored big time with her. Saw her little tight ass strolling down Telegraph one morning, dark shades, designer backpack, high heels.

"A dentist?"

"Yeah. What of it? I like teeth. I like to see a girl with a nice set. You have a nice set."

"Wow. Thanks, I guess. No one's ever picked me up with a line like that."

We got married three months later, and a year after that my father's heart stopped beating while he was showing some middle-aged couple a house over in La Costa. He told them they needed "some time alone to think it over" and left them inside to talk about the spacious dining room and Jacuzzi tub. My dad went outside and keeled over into the pool. They never heard him, so he drowned before CPR could save his life. Morons.

An old Chinese dentist retired his practice to me for a good price. Easy street. Kate, his dental hygienist, stayed on, but I needed another girl for the front desk. Two days later the ad paid off. I narrowed it down to two: Elly and Barbara. Both were smart. Both were cute. Both seemed like they'd be good with impatient people who might be waiting for a doctor who often ran twenty minutes behind schedule. But Elly had a better set. She obviously flossed. She got the job.

I went to see Al, usually when Jessica was out of town. She was gone on Tuesday, so I locked up, grabbed a bite at La Paloma, and pulled into the parking lot. Scrubbed hallways, white shiny floors, yellow and pink walls, the smell of disinfectant crammed up against pee. I held my breath for an hour. Bodies sat in wheelchairs and flowered couches, in the corners, in their rooms on their flat beds, in the lounge, heads hung on failing necks. Wrinkled hands reaching out to fix a loose string. I couldn't stand it. I couldn't stand to watch my grandfather, an old man with yellowed teeth, snort through his nose tubes at *Happy Days*. Chachi was proposing marriage to Joanie. I held the plastic cup full of beef consommé while he sucked at the straw. I laughed at the television when he did.

I couldn't wait for him to die.

I thought about having sex with Jess. She was coming home tonight. It'd been weeks since we'd made love. I got a hard-on sitting there next to Al.

"I'm late," she said.

I looked at her as she got up from the bed. I stretched my arms up over my head and pulled my back into alignment. "What are you talking about?" I was worn out. I wanted to roll over and fall asleep.

"My period. I haven't gotten it for a while. I'm pretty sure I'm pregnant."

"Pretty sure?"

"Okay. Totally sure." She stopped unpacking her suitcase and sat down on the bed by my feet. "It's been a few weeks along. I guess I wasn't paying attention."

I grabbed her around that tiny waist of hers and pulled her back with me. Her hair flowed around the pillow. I beamed a smile at the side of her face.

"Alan. We're going to name him Alan, for my dad, okay?"

She pushed herself out of my arms and stood up, went into the bathroom. What the fuck was she doing?

"I don't want this baby," I thought I heard her say. I went into the bathroom and watched her sit on the toilet to pee.

"What? I'm not following you," I said.

She tugged her red silk robe off the hook behind the door and walked out. I caught my reflection in the mirror as I followed. My stomach sagged a little. I grimaced.

"Jess, baby. What are you talking about? Are you worried about your body? You are going to look so hot pregnant. We can make the office into a nursery to start—"

"Not yet. No," she said, shaking her head. "I want to do more with my job first. I want to see where it goes. A baby's just gonna kill it for me right now."

I wanted to kill her. "So what? You're going to kill the baby instead? Please, let's talk about it." I was angry. I was starting to feel like I could hit her. But I'd never do that. Never done that. Never would. I shoved on my underwear and walked back into the bathroom, closed the door, clenched my fist, and punched the wall instead. WHAP! I did it again.

"Scott, what are you doing in there?" she asked the door.

"Nothing. Just saw the medicine cabinet was a little loose, so I banged it back into the wall," I lied. Then I sat on the edge of the tub and held my aching fist to my stomach.

"Scott? I need you to know. I'm doing it tomorrow at ten, if you want to come."

I got up and opened the door. I knew from her face there was no way I could change her mind. "Please don't. Please," I begged. Hugged her against me. "It doesn't have to be a big deal. We can afford help. You take a little time off from your job—"

She shrugged away from me hard. It felt like I was dropping a bag of groceries. "You're not listening to me, Scott. I really am not having a baby right now. The timing is bad. Jacques says that if I keep it up, the way I'm going, I'll be division head by next year."

"Sounds like you've given this a lot of thought." I walked to the window. Outside, the moon made jagged shavings on the pool. "What else can I say?" So much for easy street.

I went downstairs and out the sliding door to the backyard. I took off my briefs and dove into the water. For a fleeting moment I remembered my mother dunking me in and out of the ocean. I was four when she died, so I probably made it up. I came to the surface and leaned my elbows up over the edge of the pool onto the cement. My head pulsed. A cold breeze tore into my chest.

I called her at home the next day around three o'clock. No answer. I told Kate to polish Mrs. Schuler's teeth. Asked Elly to cancel the rest of the day, and I drove home.

She was lying on the bed. A glass of water on the nightstand and a bottle of Advil. Another bottle too. I recognized the yellow of a prescription bottle. Antibiotics.

"You did it, didn't you?"

She turned her head sideways, her pale skin almost disappeared against the beige sheets. I wanted it to. Wanted it gone. She didn't look meek enough for me. No big sorry frown. She'd already gone beyond it.

"Scott. Honey. Please don't be mad at me." She sat up and put a shaky hand across her belly. Empty belly. My kid. Wiped out. Clean.

"How can you ask that? I am so fucking pissed off right now. I hate you, you know." I looked out the window at the pool. I loved her. I couldn't live without her.

"No, you don't." I could feel her looking at me. Feel her trying to get me to look at her. "Scott, we just moved here. You just started a new practice. I've got this totally great job. Why do we have to rush into having kids? We're both still so young."

"You're young. I'm almost forty."

"Thirty-three is not almost forty. Now come here and let me kiss you," she purred.

I turned and looked at her. "Are you feeling okay?" I had to be sure she wasn't going to die.

"I'm actually fine. Just some cramping." She cocked her head sideways like a puppy. "Maybe you could make me some soup?"

She was kidding, right? She kills my kid and wants me

to feed her? Something in me tilted to the side and for a moment I felt like I could have shoved her face into the pillow and made her gasp for life.

"You know, Jess, I need to get out of here," I grumbled. I wanted some time not looking at her face. "I'm going back to the office."

Elly was there finishing up filing the patient records. I asked her, "Any problems with the cancellations?"

"Not really. Just Bob Rice. He's an incredibly unpleasant man. But I told him I could squeeze him in tomorrow, so he cooled off."

"Great." I needed a distraction. Maybe I needed to get even. "Want to get a drink?" I asked.

She looked at me, startled. "You're married."

I laughed. "Well, yes I am, but that never stopped me from having a life."

We went to the sports pub down the street. Season Ticket. I liked the name. We sat at a round table in the back below a television set on mute. We both ordered beer. The place smelled like hot dogs.

"What's a smart girl like you doing working in a dentist's office? You just got your degree. You've got looks. You could do anything."

She blushed. That excited me.

"I was looking for a job, not a career. I'm saving all the money I make for Europe. I want to be gone by next spring."

I wanted her to squirm. "So you lied to me. You said you were looking for a long-term deal."

She didn't take the bait. "Oh well. You want to let me go now because I might not be around in six months? Go for it. I could find plenty of stupid receptionist jobs."

"Yeah? Why'd you pick my job?"

"You were the cutest doctor I interviewed with."

Now I was the one blushing. "Really? You're that shallow?"

"No, I was kidding," she said, laughing.

That pissed me off. I know I'm good-looking. I wanted her to think so.

"Look. You are cute. Totally cute. But you're married." She held her pint glass in two hands and thumbed the rim slowly back and forth.

"And you're a kid. What are you, twenty?"

"Twenty-three in two months. Not a kid, thank you very much, Mr. Mature Dentist Man." She was flirting with me.

I kept her sitting there in front of me in that hard wooden chair for two hours. I ordered her another beer, then another. Plied her with questions about her life. Typical smart-ass, a lot like me. Normal fucked-up family life. Went to college far away and now she's home again. Saving her money. Waiting for her adventures to start.

"Look," she said, a glass shy of total embarrassment. "Uh. I'm a little drunk and I'm thinking maybe you should—"

"Drive you home? No problemo. Where do you live?"

She weaved a bit when she stood up and made for the front door. "Off Poinsettia Lane. Do you know where that is?"

"Sure," I said.

We got into my Celica and I drove 78 West. I exited in Carlsbad and headed south along Carlsbad Boulevard.

"This is the longest way to my parents' house you could have taken," she said.

I wanted some more of her. I felt like I had the right to. "I know. Thought we'd catch a sunset. Do you mind?"

"Not a bit." She slumped back comfortably in the soft leather bucket seat. I pulled off where Batiquitos Lagoon and the Pacific Ocean touch noses. The rocky beach in front of us was empty except for a few gulls scrounging their last meals before the sun went down. The waves were loud with the windows down. My left hand rested on my side-view mirror and my right on the armrest between us. The sun was just about to hit the horizon.

"I heard that if you stare really hard at the sun at the

exact moment it meets the ocean, you'll see a flash of green,"
Elly said. Her speech was less slurred than I'd wanted it to be.

"Huh," I said. I was bored. I thought about Jess. First
I smiled. Then I remembered. "Want to walk?" I didn't wait
for an answer and got out of the car. I knew she'd follow.

We walked across the rocks, our arms outstretched for
balance, and landed on the soft flat sandy ground by the edge
of the bubbling water. We both put our hands in our coat
pockets. The wind picked up slightly and she shivered audibly.
I made my move. Put my arm around her. One second. Two.
Three.

"Hello?" She looked at me.

Dammit.

"What?" I played stupid. "Thought you were cold."

She didn't move away. Skip to my Lou.

I kissed her. She kissed me back. Tasted good. Like
beer and jasmine. I like a clean mouth.

She laughed. "I can't believe you just kissed me. You
are insane." She kept laughing. She was uncomfortable, but
pretending to be cool, mature. I pushed the envelope, pulled
her down to the beach with me. Me on my back, her on top,
her face falling into mine, me kissing her again, rubbing her
back under her coat, her sweater, the shirt under that. No bra.
I moved my hand in front. Squeezed her small breast.

She put her arms down on each side of my head.

Straightened up, but kept her lower body pressed against mine. I bet she felt me hard. "What the hell are we doing? This is bad." But she was still smiling. She liked it. Liked me. I liked her back. This was fun city.

"Shut up and kiss me some more," I said, and nudged her arms enough to make them give way. She fell forward. I caught her shoulders and let her mouth fall on top of mine.

I took her home when we both got too cold to kiss anymore. She thanked me and said she'd get a ride to work tomorrow with her dad. She bent low after she closed the door, shook her finger at me through the window like I was a bad boy, and walked off.

During the next week we went out three more times after work. Same place. Same beer. Same hot dog smell.

"What does your wife say about your not coming home after work?" Elly asked me on Thursday, a bite of a club sandwich still in her mouth.

Jessica hadn't said anything about my not coming home in the evenings. She hadn't noticed. She'd been working through dinners, staying in her office past primetime, sometimes until midnight. If she had asked, I would have told her I was with my grandfather. But she didn't ask. Didn't want to know what I ate for dinner. How my day went. Since the abortion we'd been doing a dance around each other like little kids on a playground, their dukes up, ready to fight, but too afraid to come closer, throw the first punch.

"She's out of town." I drank back my third beer and watched her dip a french fry in a clear plastic cup of mayonnaise. She wore khaki pants and a yellow short-sleeved cotton shirt, the tan fading from her long thin arms. She brushed some hair out of her eyes and smiled into mine. This was more fun than being pissed off at my selfish bitch wife.

I liked that I had Elly to myself 9 to 5. The office had no private examination room, just two dentist chairs, so we limited our fooling around to short stints. When Kate went out to lunch, I'd lock the door and we'd make out on one of the brown chairs. Pull the arms up, lower the head down all the way, and I'd pull her on top of me again, like at the beach. If I opened my eyes, I could see the poster of the babbling forest brook I kept for my patients to stare at while I drilled their teeth.

I found a poem Jessica had written for me on one of our anniversaries. I copied it, and put it in the front desk drawer at work for Elly.

So many times I watched the sky
Waiting for joy to fall from a star.
I searched a thousand dark skies
Before you came.
And now, in the morning

When the world is light and new
And the lonely must wait to look up
To seek their own happiness,
I look beside me and you
Are with me still. You are my joy.

On Tuesday she gave me a blow job while I was staring up at those green trees. On the same chair Mrs. Chow sat in as I fitted her for a crown forty-five minutes later.

By the following week I started calling Elly at her parents' house after saying good night to her in the Season Ticket parking lot. I needed to know what she was doing when she wasn't in my sight. If Jess was still at work, we spoke long into the night. I laughed at her bad jokes.

"Why did the guru refuse novocaine when he went to his dentist?"

"Why?"

"He wanted to transcend dental medication."

She asked me again about Jessica. I told her it was none of her business.

"So you're not feeling guilty about what we've done, what we're doing." She pushed me.

We hadn't done shit as far as I was concerned. "When are we going to make love?" I wanted to see how far this was going to go. The pussyfooting around each other was getting old.

. . .

"I hope you won't be too lonely while I'm gone." Jessica was packing, leaving the next day for two weeks in Czechoslovakia.

Don't worry about me, babe. I plan to make wild love to my receptionist while you're gone. You don't mind, do you? I watched her move across our bedroom, first to the closet, where she put her fingers to her mouth and thoughtfully selected a navy blue suit covered in plastic. Then she slowly rolled it and tucked it ever so gently, like a wounded kitten you'd find in the road, into the suitcase. Kept it from wrinkling that way. Smart girl, my wife. She knows her materials.

"Send my love to Al, would you." She reminded me that I hadn't seen my grandfather since I pulled Elly into my life.

"You bet." I got up and kissed the back of her neck. It smelled like chocolate. I would have pushed her up against the wall and packed myself into her as a going away present, but I was saving my strength for Elly. Finally. All the way. She said she wasn't going to make love to me in the office. I'd suggested my own bed.

"The bed where you have sex with your wife? You've got to be kidding. That's sick."

Some hotel somewhere. Where?

The phone woke me up. Jessica had it shoved into my face. "Wake up, Scott. It's the doctor at Ridgeview."

"Mr. Rusk, I'm sorry to—"

"Dr. Rusk. It's *doctor*."

"Sorry. Dr. Rusk. Your grandfather has passed. I'm terribly, terribly sorry. But I know it was expected. He left us in his sleep just a little while ago."

"Oh. Damn." Silence on the other end. She expected more from me. I looked at Jess beside me, a worried look on her face. Now she was going to have to cancel her trip. "Thank you. Thank you for the call. I'll be there soon."

Jessica postponed her trip for the memorial service. We had it on Wednesday. A few old friends of my grandfather's came to look at his body on view at the funeral home. I sat there with my teary mask on, greeting those two-faced pricks as if they were his war buddies come to pay homage. *Why didn't you visit him these past months while he sat alone in that awful room?* "Thank you for coming. Grandfather told me some great stories about your times together." I had a crick in the right side of my neck that just wouldn't go away.

We read his will. Left me everything, which was nothing. Some jewelry. An old Japanese scroll he had hung in his room at the nursing home. Said something about peace. Jessica wanted to hang it in our living room. I said no, I wanted to hang it at the office. Figured Elly would dig it.

Grandfather wanted to be cremated. Burnt to smithereens. Fine. Also wanted the ashes spread around the desert, his favorite place to hike, at least until he was too old to skirt the nasty cholla spines. When I was a kid both Alans took me there in the spring when the wildflowers went crazy, as if the specks of rain that had fallen the previous months were filled with some magical potion. Everywhere you looked, carpets of yellow, blue, and white flowers. I remember the ocotillo blossoms shooting off the edges of the branches like the dark red tips of wooden matches about to burst into flames.

It would be a good place to have sex with Elly.

"You want me to spread your grandfather's ashes with you? Well. Okay. That sounds pretty romantic." She laughed on the phone and I knew it was a done deal. Put your John Hancock right here.

The urn, Elly, and I checked into the Oasis Motel on Saturday afternoon. I wanted the remains out of the way, so we laced up our hiking boots and set out on the Palm Canyon Trail. October isn't the best time to see flowers; the cold air hung about the dried ground like some frangible mist. With Elly ahead of me on the trail, her long dark braid of hair bouncing against her red sweatshirt, I felt a little like those two kids in the fairy tale who dropped bread crumbs as their mother dragged them into the forest: even within the grasp of fear, they wanted to believe they would find their way back home.

We climbed along the mostly dry creek bed and stopped where the palm trees swayed over a large pool and sat on a huge white boulder together. "My dad and my grandfather loved this spot," I told Elly. "In the spring and summer there are usually about fifty people here. We'd take a water break on our way up the trail, watch all the little kids swim in the pool. The creek is really low now, but after the rains start, the creek fills up the pool. The water runs so loudly, you can hardly hear people talk."

"It's amazing. Thanks for showing it to me," Elly said. I was happy I was sharing it with Elly. Jessica would have bitched the whole time up the trail. "How much farther? My feet hurt. You know how I hate to sweat." She wasn't a fan of the great outdoors. No way she would get off on the desert. Elly's excitement was a real turn-on. Everything about Elly lately was a real turn-on.

We walked another two miles up the canyon. It was illegal what I was doing, so I looked around for potential witnesses. I thought I saw a roadrunner, but couldn't be sure. I took the maple scattering urn filled with Grandpa Alan's ashes out of the pack. Pried open the lid and shook out what was left of his old body over the parched ground. A slight breeze carried his bones across the spikes of a squat barrel cactus. Flecks of him settled quietly on the creek and moved on. Before I knew it, I started to cry; there had been too much loss. The bread crumbs had all been eaten.

"Oh, Scott. I'm so sorry you're sad." I'd made her cry. Made her move beside me and wrap her arms tight around my waist, her face pressed up against the side of my neck. She was beautiful. It felt good to stir her. She was easy that way. Always on the verge of some new emotion, like being inside of a carnival funhouse. There was no telling with Elly. I didn't doubt she cared about me, maybe loved me. But she'd been talking a lot about leaving on her trip, about a future that didn't have my name included. I needed to change that. Standing there surrounded by the mesquite, the quiet, I made some vows to myself.

Screwing her was great. I couldn't get enough of her, I devoured her. She had her period, wanted to hold off, but I said no. Insisted. We used the white towels hanging on the metal racks in the bathroom. On the bed. The floor. Didn't want to stain the sheets. We left the motel the next morning and Elly looked back into the room one last time, the twisted-up pile of bloodied towels in the corner.

"Looks like someone got murdered," she said.

A few weeks after I scattered my grandfather's ashes over the dried-out ground outside Borrego Springs, Jessica arrived home from Prague, unpacked, made herself a cup of coffee, and sat down at her small cherrywood desk to go through the mail. I came home from the office three hours later. She was waiting for me.

· · ·

It was on my face the next morning.

"What's the matter?" Elly begged.

"Jessica saw the phone bill and wanted to know why I called one number so much. She traced it. She wanted to know who in the Fisher household I called so many nights a week. I had to tell her you're my receptionist."

"It's a toll call? Shit. What else did you tell her?"

"I said we've become good friends, that's all. But she said that if we were such good friends, then she should meet you too. She said my friends should be her friends."

"What does that mean?" she asked cautiously.

"It means I'm supposed to invite you to dinner this weekend."

"Yeah, right," she whispered. Kate was in the back. "Look, Scott. No way I'm doing this. I'm going to quit instead. Here." She picked up a pen and started writing on a prescription pad. "I am formally giving you my two-weeks' notice."

I panicked. Sonofabitch! Trapped. I wanted to punch the wall. I wanted somebody hurt. I didn't want her going anywhere. I wanted it to stay the same. Jessica on one end. Elly on the other. But no touching. Now it was like tin cans attached to a string, me in the middle trying to keep them from hearing each other.

I pulled her up from the desk. Hard. Dragged her outside with me. Slammed the door.

"Scott, what are you doing?" She wasn't the least bit

scared. Not like at the beginning, when I was in charge. No. She had a cocky little look on her face. She knew what I wanted. She knew I wanted her.

I talked carefully. "Elly. I do not want to lose Jessica. I do not want to lose you."

"But if you had to make a choice?"

"What? You're asking me to leave my wife?"

I looked past her and saw my 9:00 root canal pull into the parking lot.

At lunchtime Kate ate her stinking tuna sandwich at her desk and Elly left while I was finishing polishing Mrs. Jacobs. She left before we could talk. I called that night when Jessica was in the shower. Her mother said she was out.

The next morning I came in and saw Kate looking over the shoulder of some ugly chick with big breasts who was sitting in Elly's chair. They both looked up at me like I was pointing a gun at them. "Who are you?" I asked.

"This is Cindy," Kate said. "She's a temp. Elly called for one yesterday. I guess she quit."

I went over to my desk and called her at home. No answer.

Jess was in a red negligee that night when I got home. "We haven't made love in ages, you know. What's gotten into you?" I covered my tension. Zipped it up like a coroner closing the body bag over the victim of a high-speed car crash. She dropped to her knees and undid my belt. God, I loved this woman. She was enough for me. Fuck Elly. We made love missionary style for a while. Jess looked me in the eyes. She mouthed, "I love you." I pulled out, turned her over, looked down at my cock. For a second I saw it again covered in Elly's blood.

I mailed Elly a card the next day. On the cover was a photograph of an eagle flying away toward distant mountains. Inside it said, I MISS YOU ALREADY. I added my own note too.

> Elly, you were the first thing I thought of when I woke up this morning. You want me to make a choice between you and Jessica. I can't leave Jessica. Maybe it'd be best if I didn't think of you anymore. Or then again, maybe not. Oh how I lust for the very smell of you. I will hope for a time when we can be together again. Maybe for a lifetime.

I left another message with her mother the next day. "Tell her hi." *Tell her if she doesn't call me back, I'm going to come over there and rip her throat out.*

"When are we having your good friend Elly over for dinner?" Jessica asked days later. It was raining, the drops hit the window like pebbles, rubbing against my skin.

"Never. She quit. Left me with a million files to deal with."

"Just like that? No notice?" Jessica put her fork down. "Did something upset her? Did she get another job?"

"What? No. Nothing happened." The rain made my temples hurt. "She and her boyfriend went up to Canada for some camping trip."

She tugged at me like I was a cuticle on her finger. "She has a boyfriend? You didn't know she had these plans? Why would you hire someone so irresponsible? I don't understand you, Scott. You said she was great at the office. You said you were friends—"

"Jessica." I looked at her across the table. Gave her my best nonchalant look I could. "She's a kid. How was I supposed to know she was such a flake? Case closed."

I went to Elly's house the next morning before work. Parked across the street and watched the windows, waiting. I didn't see my wife's black BMW parked down the street.

I called her again. Her father got on the phone. "Elly moved up to Marin with a friend. Her mother and I would appreciate it if you would please stop calling here." I asked for her new address. "Elly asked that we not give it to you. I'm sorry. Good-bye." *Ever feel what it's like getting your molar drilled without gas, asshole?*

I went to our bar at lunch. Drank five beers and went home. Sat at Jessica's desk, my knees banged up against the bottom. Opened the top right drawer and took out a couple of sheets of the stationery with cornflowers along the border.

I didn't hear her get out of bed.

Didn't hear the red arm on the mailbox squeal down into place.

I didn't hear the sound of the gold chain, *plink*, being pulled on the brass desk lamp.

I didn't hear her pull her suitcase out of the closet.

I saw her sitting on the edge of the bed. Dressed. Ready to go. "What's up? You going on another trip?"

"Yes. You need help, Scott. I've been following you, you know. I've watched you stalk her."

"What are you talking about?" I mean, that bitch slit my heart open. Couldn't Jess cut me a break here? "I'm not the one who killed our baby!"

"Is that what this was about? That's such bullshit, Scott. I found this letter. The one you wrote to your former receptionist, your good friend. You know, you're sick.

" 'Dear Elly.' " She snapped the pages back. The crinkle sound landed in my groin. " 'It's been a hard time for me the last few weeks. I don't want you to worry about me or what might happen. After we talked the other day, I thought a lot about it. I was ready to leave my devoted wife on the slightest reassurance from you.' " Jess looked up from the letter at me.

"Let me have that," I said weakly, knowing it was use-less. My muscles felt taut and weak, both. Like I could reach out and strangle her if I could only muster the strength.

" 'I have mourned a lot about things we never did to-gether,' " she continued. " 'And I thought that there are still things to do. I love you. Don't be afraid of that. Don't be afraid of touching me again. I'll hold you if you want or I'll let you alone. My eyes are open now. Are you playing with me? Just be honest! I don't understand. I beg you to hear me. Do you think I'm such a fool as to believe that we'll be together again? Elly, I know this was a one-shot deal. I dream some-times that after your trip you'll come back. That things here will be different. Don't think for a second that I'm scheming to get you back. I know you don't want that. I don't fit your ideal. Right? Did your parents tell you to forget me? Is that who made you run away?' " Jessica started crying.

"Fuck you. It hasn't been that easy being nice to you after what you did. I guess you can't see that." I jumped out of bed and grabbed my shirt and pants and went into the bathroom, sat down on the floor. My head in my hands. The cold tile burned me.

" 'I come to your home at night,' " Jessica yelled through the door. She wanted to torture me more. I knew I could get up, open the door, put my hands around her tiny neck, squeeze—

" 'I stop and bow low before your window. I see you in

there. Asleep. I come close to your bed and watch you in silence. I wish you are mine. Only mine. I've removed my clothes and I fall upon you. You are awake and there is terror on your face. You pull away beneath me, but I hold you down for as long as I need to. You laugh at me, but I take the pillow and make you stop. I've said enough.' "

That was the end of the letter. Now that I'd heard it read aloud, I thought I'd better get dressed and get it back in the mailbox before the mailman came. I wanted Elly to know she could always come back to me. The letter was on the bed.

I didn't hear the front door close.

Bars

SINCE ELLY HAD returned from her four-month adventure overseas, everyone and everything seemed a little duller. She had traveled to Europe with a daydream tucked inside her Kelty backpack; over there she would meet a remarkable man who had everything in common with her, and by falling in love she would have part of her future (at least the relationship part) figured out. Instead, she was back home in Carlsbad, living with her parents again and supervising telemarketers at an alternative energy company in downtown San Diego. At twenty-four she resented sitting across the table from her mother every morning eating rice cakes and drinking tea. She knew she ought to do more hands-on work in an environmental field, just as she presumed there was more to her social existence than going on Saturday afternoon hikes with the Sierra Club, or eating dinner in front of the television.

. . .

Tom was excited. He was in charge of a new project in a new town. He had found a room to rent in a small house by the beach in Mission Bay. His landlord and roommate, Andrea, was an incredibly nice, down-to-earth woman. She wore her graying hair in long braids and drank about twenty shots of espresso a day. Sure, she was fifty-five—too old to introduce him to any women his own age—but she quickly became a confidante. Almost a substitute mom. But then again, the dog down the street could have been that too. His childhood left a lot to be desired. In his early twenties he started going to meetings. Twice a week he drove to the Portland YMCA and sat on the hard metal chairs. He learned quickly from Adult Children of Alcoholics that it really was okay to be selfish, to not always be the enabler. To take for himself. And take is what he, at last, intended to do. He had just gotten his Ph.D. and now was in charge of a research post at the famous San Diego Zoo. He knew what was to come after: an adventure or two in the field, then a good job with decent pay. At some point along the way, he'd find a wife. Have a real family. He wanted someone he could trust. He wanted to come home and not have to clean vomit off the bathroom floor.

She'd never thought of herself as out-and-out sexy, perhaps just a bit on the captivating side. Long thick brown hair, bangs just flirting with her eyelids. No makeup, usually, but now and then she brushed some mascara on her lashes because her mother once told her it made her brown eyes look that much larger. She fitted her thin legs into black jeans and put on a gray cashmere sweater. She looked into the mirror as she hitched the back of a string of pearls together around her neck. She checked her teeth for any sign of food, sighed, and got into her car for the drive to the Hilton to meet Barry from accounting. He had asked her to join him at the new dance club. A new place to check out sounded great. "I'd love to," Elly responded, honestly happy to go, even if she was not at all attracted to Barry. He was quite sweet, with his blue eyes and freckles. A young Ron Howard–type.

Work took up most of Tom's time. Afterward, he would come home and go for a run in the autumn twilight, and maybe grab a sandwich at the sub shop down the street. If Andrea were home they would sometimes sit together in the tiny garden out back and talk; he with a juice in his hand, she with yet another small cup of dark espresso in hers. "Why on earth are you spending your nights with your old landlord, instead of being out there having fun, meeting women?" Andrea asked him. He admitted that there were a few cute girls working at the zoo, sure, but he wasn't really interested in getting involved with anyone yet, or at least that's what he thought his plan ought to be. He thought about the teasingly funny biodiversity consultant from up north whom he spoke with a couple of times on the phone. The girl, Marnie, had asked him what he did at night and he didn't know why, but he lied to her; told her that he was dating a few different women at the moment.

Maybe Barry is more exciting out of the office than he comes off at work, Elly suggested to herself as she pulled into the Hilton parking lot. Once again she was mad at herself for agreeing to go out with someone just to see if she could possibly make him live up to some potential she envisioned; weld him into some semblance of the dream man she had pictured, as if a metallurgist. She twisted the knot from the side of her neck and reached for the door.

"Have you heard of that new dance club that opened up at the beachside Hilton?" Tom overheard on Friday as he munched a tuna sandwich while sitting on a park bench. The pigeons noticed his droppings but the two twenty-something women sitting on the next bench over did not. As they got up to leave, to trudge slowly back to their office jobs, he heard the scrape of sheer stockings against their inner thighs. He felt an erec-

tion beneath the confines of his jeans, so he crossed his legs
and starved for the few minutes it took the girls to pass by.

Elly saw Barry dancing with a young woman in a green sleeveless
dress. They looked good together dancing, their heads nodding
up and down in synch. Elly smiled when she caught his eye
and waved. He said something to the girl, who looked obviously
disappointed, and ran to meet Elly at the bar. "Hi," he said,
breathing hard from dancing. "I got here a while ago. I hope
you don't mind I started without you." Elly laughed and told
him that he looked like he was having a blast with that girl.
Barry said, "I am. She's a friend of my sister's. We haven't
seen each other in years. It's really weird meeting her here like
this. I used to have such a crush on her." A surge of relief
pressed against Elly. She looked at her watch. "I really can't
stay long, anyway," she said. "Why don't you go hang out with
her and we can get together another night, okay?" She watched
him run back to the dance floor and smile at the girl in the
green dress. The bartender asked her if she wanted a drink.
"A piña colada, please," she said.

Standing at the bar of the dance club in the Hilton, Tom
ordered a tonic water with lime. He loved to suck the tartness

from the fruit, then gulp the icy bubbles immediately after. It gave his throat a rush. Looking around the room he watched the couples and singles talking, dancing, passing business cards, drinking colored liquid from red and white striped straws. The music had a nice beat and he shifted back and forth in time with the drums' rhythms. A large man in a blue blazer bumped him while reaching for his beer on the bar behind Tom, causing him to look to his right. He noticed the girl in the gray cashmere sweater immediately. He liked the way the soft material hugged her small breasts and showed off their pertness. She was watching the dancers on the floor and moving her hips right and left to the music. He was about to move toward her when a tall thin blond guy walked up to her. Tom watched her shrug her shoulders, nod yes, and walk out to the dance floor with him.

"Hi," Elly said, after running her fingers through her bangs. Finally, she thought, he came up to her. She'd noticed him while she was dancing with Randy, the tall blond who worked at a savings and loan and who wouldn't shut up about the Padres. She knew he was looking at her from where he stood at the bar, and she danced more provocatively for him, not for Randy. After thanking the baseball-obsessed banker, she went back to the bar and picked up her drink. He came and stood next to her. Up close he was even more good-looking. He looked to be about thirty. A small scar ran from the corner of his right eye up to the tip of his eyebrow. Dressed in blue jeans and a white Oxford shirt. His brown hair was straight and cut like a little boy's, but his face showed maturity. His posture was almost too perfect. Like he was carrying something heavy inside.

They danced two fast dances together, looking directly at each other, touching casually now and then. The third song was slow and he held her close and moved easily with her arms around the small of his back. He liked the way she smelled, like something a rich older woman would spritz on herself while staying at her country home. It was a musky smell mixed with the scent of Earl Grey tea. The band took a break. "Do you want to take a walk and look at the water?" Tom asked. He wanted to get her outside, away from the possibility of another tall blond asking her to dance. She said yes.

"I'm doing a short-term research project on the mating habits of primates in captivity, but I'm hoping to be off within the year to study orangutans in their natural habitat," he told her as they walked along the pier at the back of the hotel. Elly was completely attracted to this guy and what he did for a living. A scientist. Nature. Travel. Adventure. She vaguely heard him say he would be leaving within the year. She wondered if he was a good kisser. In the harbor in front of them the boats clanged.

It was too bad this pretty woman had no profession to speak of, but her interest in the natural world seemed sincere. Obviously smart, she worked for a solar energy company and wanted to do something more in the environmental area, but figured she had to go to graduate school first. "I didn't do that well on the GRE tests," she admitted. "I'd like to think I can still find a job or a program or something that doesn't require filling in the correct circle." God, he wanted to kiss her and he had known her for only an hour. Her enthusiastic way of describing her passions about the outdoors made him smile. Tom listened on, but paid more attention to her eyes and mouth than to her actual words.

During her drive home she smiled out the rolled-down window of the car, her hair whipping back. Tom had walked her to her car, and promised to call the phone number on the scrap of paper she handed him. After a perfunctory hug, he moved his mouth to her face and gave her the slightest kiss about a millimeter shy of her lips. Her mother came into the bathroom while she was washing up. "He's smart and handsome and into animals and, oh man, what a body," she said to her mother's reflection in the bathroom mirror. "Just be careful, sweetheart," her mother warned as she closed the door and left Elly to brush her teeth. "You just met him and already you're planning your wedding. Just don't get your hopes up so much."

"She's really pretty and I think I even felt her purr while we were slow dancing," Tom told Andrea, who was still up watching television when he got home. "I know it's too soon to tell, but there's just something so magical about her, the way she walks, the way she dances, the things she says. I can't believe we met in a bar. What kind of story is that to tell our kids?" Andrea flipped off the television and sat up straight against the back of the couch. "Come here. Sit." She patted the seat next to her. "Tom. Tom. Tom." She smiled, her lips a tight line. "Far be it from me to tell you how to live your life, particularly your love life. I mean, being divorced three times doesn't exactly make me an expert. But didn't you tell me no more than two weeks ago that you're out of here by the summer? That your job is your life right now?" Andrea tried to rub some sense into his head. "I know you want to settle down one day, but honey, just go easy on yourself. See what there is to see."

. . .

The next month was sweet. She got letters from him in the mail, even though they lived thirty minutes apart. He met Elly's parents, Helen and Jerry, who had mixed reactions to the five-minute meeting: "He's very tall," her mother commented. "I didn't like the way he shook my hand. Too flimsy for a big man," her father complained. Elly didn't care; she loved Tom's strength and loved even more the way he held her hand as they walked through the hidden parts of the zoo where tourists aren't allowed to go. In the back pens she saw a baby penguin and a young ocelot. He showed her the food preparation area, where she turned up her nose at the smell of meat and fish snacks. It was hard to get together during the week, but on the weekends they hiked or hung out on the beach, and at night went dancing at the Belly Up Tavern in Solana Beach. They talked about making love, but he told her he wanted to wait, to get to know her a little more. Still, she shaved her legs each day in anticipation.

He wanted desperately to make love to her, and wasn't sure why he was putting her off. Something told him to wait. To be sure. He toured her around the zoo and let her sit in his tiny office while he went to a grant meeting. He did not hear a word anyone said and thought only of their planned lunch together. They walked to his bench in the park and he handed

her the cellophane-wrapped avocado and cheese sandwich he
had made for her that morning.

She could taste the curry powder he'd sprinkled on the sandwich. It was delicious. He was delicious. Almost five weeks of
seeing each other and she predicted that they were on their
way to something serious; she felt it in her bones like an old
sailor feels a storm coming in from the north. This weekend
they would make love. They would start planning their future
together.

Their bodies meshed like they had when they danced together
that first night. He satisfied her first, knowing it would make
a difference to Elly. She reveled in anything he did that showed
he cared for her specifically. Not that he considered himself a
selfish lover, but he had in the past often breezed over what
he thought of as the minutiae of lovemaking, heading straight
for the final rush. But with Elly he took his time, feeling out
her body's every cleft with his tongue and hands. In rhythmic
balance they arched their bellies toward each other, her legs
tight around his hips. Afterward, he lay down beside her,
watching her sleep as the light from the streetlamp crossed her
reddened cheek.

• • •

"Good morning. You must be Andrea," Elly said, looking up from her cup of coffee. She watched the older woman take out coffee beans from the freezer and put them in a white grinder. The clattering of the beans and the high-pitched whir of the machine echoed off the blue walls of the kitchen. Elly wanted to crawl back to bed, but not without Tom in it. Every Saturday morning the zoo held a Sunrise Surprise Stroll, and Tom led that week's group as the designated educator. She had meant to leave the house when he did, but he insisted she not rush out. "It's Saturday. Have some coffee and read the paper. If you meet a strange woman, that's my landlady. She's nice. Don't worry about it," he said, before taking off with the rising sun at his back. Andrea sat down across from Elly and opened the business section of the newspaper. "It's nice to finally meet you," Elly said. Andrea smiled at her for a moment then looked down and scanned the stocks. Elly figured it best not to make conversation. She timidly pulled the comics toward her and they drank quietly in the slightly uncomfortable silence.

Tom bent down to pick up the sheaf of papers that had fallen off his desk, and noticed the research grant pamphlet sticking out. If he got the grant, he would leave for the Pittsburgh Zoo in July for preliminary research. Then Borneo in the fall.

Only two months as lovers and Elly was already talking about joining him on the field study to Borneo. The grant would not pay for two. They would have to be married for that to happen. But there was no way he was ready for such a commitment. This trip was all that mattered to him, he realized with a snap of honesty he'd been ignoring the last few sexually-fulfilling weeks. Yeah, he liked Elly; thought she was a great lover and fun to hang out with. But marriage? When he first met Elly, he'd talked casually to Andrea about having children with her, but now he got anxious when Elly kidded him about the beautiful children they would have together. Smart, funny, and interesting, Elly could be the woman of his dreams, someday in the future. But not now. If she couldn't come to Borneo, he wondered, would their relationship stand up after a year's absence? Would she even be there to say good-bye to him at the airport? Would he want her there upon his return? Too many uneasy questions arising. He needed some distance. Some perspective. He got up and went outside to check on Sonya, the female orangutan.

Elly wasn't sure Tom felt as strongly about her as she did him. She was almost in love. Sure, there were some difficulties; his emotions never lingered too long on one street. It made her dizzy at times. He was sweet and nurturing, but he was also maddeningly self-protective. At times he would be lighthearted and generous with his laughter, while at other times he could be dangerously detached. It was during one of his cold episodes that she suspected their relationship was not as perfect for either of them as she imagined it to be. They made love. More quickly than usual; instead of their usual twenty minutes of kissing and touching, he wanted to be inside her almost immediately. Afterward, he got up from the bed and said he was going to make himself a piece of toast with butter and honey. "That sounds so good," she said, a tired smile on her face. "I'd like some tea with mine." He turned and looked at her after putting on his boxer shorts. "Elly, I really want to get something to eat right now. If you want some tea, could you maybe get up and make it yourself?"

On December 15, he was notified that the Wildlife Foundation of Indonesia had awarded him the grant. The idea of working alongside famed orangutan researcher Birute Galdikas thrilled him to no end. The rumor was that she had left behind her own child in Canada to stay in the tropics and fight for the survival of the orangutans amidst falling trees and land-grabbing international corporations, in his mind a heroic and unselfish act. It would be nice, he knew, to have both a healthy career and satisfying relationship. But his instincts told him to stop asking for the whole oyster and be glad he just got the pearl.

• • •

"Hi, Andrea. This is Elly. Any chance we can meet for coffee?"

He sat at the kitchen table watching Andrea stir the bubbling tomato sauce in the copper pot. "She really fell for you, you know," Andrea said to him. He could tell she was trying to make him feel bad. It made him somewhat angry that Elly got Andrea involved. "What is it you want me to do?" he asked her. "I like her. She's amazing. But she is too ready, too unbelievably sure that we should be together forever. That she could be my research partner. I'm not really in need of one right now. She needs to get her own life, you know?"

Elly looked at the older woman across from her, a woman who knew the man in her life. "There's a side of my brain that thinks we're not really right for each other," she admitted. "But we are so good together in so many ways." She watched Andrea take out a clove cigarette and light it. Elly continued, "I just think if we had more time, we'd know. He thinks I'm rushing things, but he's leaving in a few months." She sighed and waited for a response. Andrea blew a puff of smoke over her right shoulder. "Since you've asked me what I think you should do, I'm going to tell you. I think you should take on a project of your own. Get involved. Go to school, I don't know. Something. Something that'll make him think he's not your whole life." She took a sip of her double espresso. Elly thought this over for a moment. "But he is my whole life right now." She wasn't sure what Andrea was getting at. "What's the matter with that?" Andrea stubbed out the cigarette under her sandal and wrapped the butt in a napkin. "You don't get it, do you?" She sighed. "Tom is most attracted to women who are independent like he is. When he first met you, he was thrilled that you had these goals to do something more. Now you're telling him your only goal is to be with him. Does that make sense?"

Now that he knew he was leaving, the relationship was going to play out like a poker game, he could tell. Eventually they would both have to stop raising each other's bets, and call. He would have to tell her no way was she going to Borneo. And she would want to know if she should bide her time until his return. Even though there was a part of him that loved the idea of a lover waiting across the time zones, pining for his touch, he had to be honest. Tell her to get on with her life. Not wrap her existence around his.

Elly looked across the table at Tom as he took a huge bite of his grilled Mahi Mahi sandwich. The hard chair she was seated in wasn't the most comfortable for a leisurely lunch by the beach, but the Poseidon Restaurant in Del Mar could get away with it; they had the spot for eating outside on a warm April day. She heard the shouts of the surfers as they caught rides on the high waves. "Guess what," she said as casually as she could. "I applied to graduate school. I didn't want to tell you until I knew for sure, but I made the application deadline and got in! Brown University, no less. There was an opening in the Environmental Studies program and I landed it. I start in the fall."

He liked that while he was gone she would be engrossed in matters other than his heart and soul. Or did he? Her attitude about him was changing before his eyes. Less dependence on his return and more on her own future. He liked that. Or did he? He would wish her luck, and maybe even visit her in Rhode Island before he left the country. See how she lived without him as an anchor for her future.

It was working. She saw the worry in his eyes. No longer would she be waiting in San Diego, working at a dead-end job, going out dancing on Friday nights. She would be starting anew, a playground of adventure without him.

. . .

The remaining few months they had together were easy on them both. She was distracted with graduate school reading lists and travel preparations. He knew that Elly still wished for some commitment from him, specifically that he come home and they get engaged, but she backed off just enough for them to enjoy lovemaking and walks on the beach without straining for a perfect sunset. When they were together, he did not fret when she took his hand in hers. He relaxed.

"Thank you, Andrea," she told her new ally on the telephone. "That was great advice. I'm so excited about going to school. I think it'll be really good for me. Have a great year and think of me this winter building snowmen and wearing wool."

She left for the East a few weeks before he did. She was gone and he missed her. He piled the cameras and tape recorder and the many empty notebooks in the corner of his room. He resealed his tent and fixed the zipper on his sleeping bag and got his tetanus shot. When he had said good-bye to her, it was at her house, not the airport. She was sad and that made his heart full. He said he would try to visit her before leaving for Borneo. He promised to be careful and to write. She had made no further demands.

· · ·

School was hard, classes were more dull than she expected, and she had few friends. In her sparsely furnished apartment she read about the effects of gold mining on rivers. Tom phoned her when he got to Pittsburgh. She tried to restrain herself. "The weather is bleak, and by the way, I miss you," she said. He told her he missed her too, and would try to visit before leaving the country. "That would be great. See if you can swing it. Even for a couple of days," she responded.

Visiting was a mistake. He knew it four seconds after he saw her by the way she hugged him at the airport, the way she held his hand and his gaze in the car to her apartment. She cried while they made love, tears fell on his chest as she moved slowly above him. "Why are you so sad?" he asked, brushing her hair away from her face, even though he already knew the answer. "I love you," she admitted, snuggling down into the crook of his arm, his chest raising her head with each strained breath. "I want us to spend our lives together. That's all there is to it," she sighed.

She felt she finally had him. He'd come out of his way for a visit; he must really want to be with her now, and hopefully, forever. She had claimed her independence, and he was responding. She had shown him she did not really need him, but that she would make room in her life for him.

• • •

What had he gotten himself into? He was bewildered. "Elly. I thought we were past the whole commitment thing," he sputtered. "I thought things were going the way we both envisioned. That I would leave for the year, but that there would be no golden promises made before I left. Did I miss something here?" He propped himself against a pillow and pulled the other one in front of his chest. Armor.

"Maybe it was me who missed something," she said, while getting dressed to leave for class. "Not ten minutes ago, just as you were about to have an orgasm, you said you loved me. Didn't you come here maybe because you do love me? I want to wait for you, Tom. I want you to want me to. Simple as that." She picked up her daypack. "I never should have said anything because now I've got to go to class. I can't miss it. Take a shower. There's some pasta in the fridge. Let's talk later." She closed the door behind her, feeling uncertainty in the pit of her stomach. On her walk back to her apartment from her Ecosystem Analysis class she sensed that he wouldn't be waiting for her.

Alone in her apartment he reenacted the scene again and again. Simple as that? She thought it was simple to say "I love you"? Simple to be able to wait a year for each other? They'd been down this road before; they'd talked countless times about his being able to go away without being constrained by her. He did love her, in some ways, but not enough to put their lives on hold for each other. He knew he couldn't continue this conversation later. He got into a taxi twenty-three minutes after she had gone.

She found his letter in her mailbox a few days later.

> Elly,
>
> Here I am leaving for Borneo in just a few days and I am in turmoil. Your insecurities about this relationship and your wanting assurances from me are driving me mad. It seems that it's been every other day when you ask me if I miss you or love you. I find it impossible to respond in the negative to such types of questions. Sometimes I feel like I have to spend so much of my time answering questions from you and convincing you that you mean something to me. I find myself wanting to convince you that I love you and that there is a future between us only to get you to stop asking.
>
> Truly, you have added pleasure to my life. I enjoyed so much of what we had together. But as you probably know, your desire for a long-term commitment has always been stronger than mine.

I want you to know that you've been a great companion for these past months, but what it comes down to is that what I want and need from you is quite different from what you want and need from me. I'm sorry if this is harsh, but I don't think you can ever be the woman I would choose to spend my life with.

I am sure this hurts you, and that's the last thing I want to do to you, but I want to make my feelings clear before I leave for Borneo. Elly, I leave with a sad heart. Sad for you. I really do hate the thought of you there in the New England cold licking your wounds and pretending you aren't. I know you are too social for that to last too long and am comforted by the image of you making your way into the hearts of your schoolmates. I adore you, Elly, but I don't think I can love you the way you want me to.

Again, I am grateful for what we've had.

Be well,
Tom

Borneo was blissful. The research at Camp Leakey satisfied him completely. For hours he sat and observed orangutans in their natural habitat. He took notes and photographs, charted data, and shared his ideas with colleagues. Martha, a rugged and tanned graduate student from Minneapolis, helped him take blood samples from pregnant females. Though not pretty like Elly, Martha's need of him was limited, finite. They made love in his tent at night and their sweat intermingled with the dew of the forest floor, the noise of the cicadas and birds a constant backdrop to their own sounds. The year went by more quickly than he'd imagined. But there was a new and exciting job waiting for him when he got back to the States. He couldn't wait to tell his former landlady, Andrea, about his appointment as the assistant director of the Wildlife Conservation Society's primate research center, through the Bronx Zoo.

She spent time with Colin, the political science major with the blond hair and feminine face, and long, soft fingers to match. He took her to dinner a few times a month and she enjoyed their talks long into the night. The chemistry between them, alas, remained elusive. Elly's heart was a colorless palette. A passable year academically with a melancholy air following her like a slow swarm of dull bees. She heard through Andrea that Tom was coming to work on the East Coast. She missed him and secretly wished the year apart might have softened his refusal of her. That last letter—he said that he wasn't sure she could be the woman of his dreams. But did that mean he wasn't still open to the possibility?

. . .

They found a small two-bedroom in a renovated brownstone on West 88th, between Columbus and Central Park West. Martha was there each night he returned home from the zoo, quietly working on her dissertation.

She wrote to him at the zoo.

Dear Tom,

Just a quick note to find out how you are doing and how the trip went. Andrea gave me this address, so I hope you don't mind me writing to you at work. Thank you for the earrings you sent me. The red and black stones are beautiful. Are they some local gemstone? It would have been nice if you'd said more in the only letter you sent me, but hey, I know you must have been really busy.

So now you're back home. Funny that you're working at a zoo again. You thought you would end up someplace totally different. People can never be sure of their tomorrows, can they? Speaking of zoos, remember how you said we made love like wild animals? I miss making love like that.

School is fine, but I am very much alone here in my tiny apartment above a noisy street. A couple moved in next door to me last month and they fight all the time. They say the harshest things to each other. Remember how you and I shared passion, even in our arguments? We never lacked passion, did we?

After all this time I have to admit that I still long for you. Maybe you'll consider coming for a visit. My address has not changed. Until then. Good luck with the new job. Be well.

Love,

Elly

I am on Bainbridge Island at my ex-boyfriend John's
house, playing catch with my ex-cat. Even though John and
I could not make a go of our love affair, we are making a real
effort to maintain a friendship. This includes me coming to
the island once in a while so that I can visit the cat we shared.
John's house—my ex-house—is perched on a cliff overlooking
Puget Sound and is surrounded by a half acre of forest. Since
my apartment in Seattle totals about 450 square feet, we had
agreed that John's house is the best place for the cat to live.

I'm holding a long branch and tossing pine cones in
the air to hit to the cat. Every now and then I connect with a
sticky cone, and when she sees it move in the air above her,
she paws at it. Then a bird cries overhead. A fat robin and she
is distracted, a very cat thing to be. Even though this is futile,
I am having fun in the clean early-afternoon air. The forest

is wet from the dew, still, and the green smell soothes me. Her back is to me this time. I call her name and hit her another cone, but she is licking her left paw.

John will be back home in a while so that he can take me to the ferry. That's the deal: when I have some free time to visit, he promises to pick me up at the ferry dock, and then drop me back at the boat after I spend some quality time with the cat. I moved off the island a few months ago, long after I had satisfied the gods and myself that I couldn't be happy here. Not with John, anyway.

The problem with John was that he worked too hard at his job. He was also incredibly fulfilled by it. I know it's selfish to say this, but at the time we were living together I didn't understand why he couldn't share the same passion for me as he did teaching acting workshops to a bunch of teenagers. When he came home at night, he worked on his next day's assignments. On weekends he fussed over his own material. I whined about being ignored. I complained also because I wasn't thrilled about my own life; the classes I took at the university weren't as inspiring as I wanted them to be. That must have rubbed off on the relationship. I can't see how it didn't.

At first we ignored the obvious, hoping it'd go away, like a large spider on the ceiling no one wants to climb on a chair to swat. But after almost two years together (one living on the island), we didn't take much more than a passing interest in each other. Implicitly we both craved more than being roommates, eating an occasional dinner together.

The cat, though. We loved the cat. She slept between us and we liked the warmth she created for our backs. So, now, when I feel like getting out of the city, I take the ferry through the mostly calm waters of Puget Sound, watching the Seattle skyline fall away into the horizon, and I even look forward to John's face, his eyes behind the steering wheel of his yellow Toyota truck as the boat docks. It's worth the ferry ride, sometimes. Seeing his face again. Seeing the cat.

This morning I took the 9:25 A.M. ferry. John said it was a good time to come because he would be directing an acting workshop over in Poulsbo, so he could drop me off, spend a couple of hours teaching people how to emote from their cores, then get me to the 2:10 ferry back to Seattle.

It's a thirty-five-minute trip on the ferry. Since it was one of those rare warm spring days, I sat outside on a green painted bench. Thirty-five minutes of peace with myself was all I asked for, but a man, too young to be balding, sat down beside me and asked me if I lived on the island. I said I did a few hundred years ago. He ignored my statement like it was some gnat flying by his face. He asked me about the price of owning a home, and did I know any of the famous artists and writers who live along the island's green shores. I said I didn't know, and no, and left the salty wind to him and the deck. I wandered inside and eyed the families going home and tourists pointing excitedly out the windows. A little girl was being led in circles around the cabin by her father. She was screaming and he must have thought this walkabout around the itchy passengers would quiet her. It made me dizzy even though it was at least three minutes between each pass. Like Chinese water torture, my body stiffly anticipated the next loud circling. I stood up to get a cup of chamomile tea, but the boat docked before I could make it to the counter.

John smiled over his steering wheel and I got in next to him. In his mild-mannered way he asked me how it was going. I told him fine, even though I had been feeling pretty isolated in my tiny apartment lately. I said that because I suffer from Goldilocks Syndrome: I want everything to be just right. We drove in silence to the white house at the end of the private road. I remembered the first time we drove down this road with the property manager. I'd sat in the backseat of the realtor's brown Buick, counting the cigarette butts on the floor. I could tell she liked us, thought we would be good tenants. We were young, in love, and had enough money to pay the rent. This apparently showed on our faces.

We had pulled up in front of a small white wooden house. Standing in the gravel-covered front yard, we could see through the front windows all the way through to the back window and out onto Puget Sound. We hadn't even walked to the front door yet when John told her we'd take the house.

Cigarette-butt lady asked, "Don't you want to see inside first?" John said, "We already did."

The cat's real name is Eloise. She's black. We call her Little Ricky, Ratface, or sometimes Boofhead. We used to try to catch fish off our beach and the one time we caught a flounder we fed the blood and guts and bones to her. She licked her paws for so long, we had to throw her outside so we could get some sleep.

I hear John's truck behind me. It's almost time for me to go home. I wave to him from the end of the long driveway and he inches the truck slowly toward me, that familiar sound on the gravel and brush beneath its tires. I used to wait hours to hear that sound during the time we spent here together. The cat and I would be playing or I would be cooking some lentil or garbanzo bean stew, the smells of turmeric and curry filling the house, and I'd hear the sound on the pebbles. John and I would go out to the porch together and drink cold beers and look out over Puget Sound, hoping to spot a whale, an eagle, a dolphin. One time we drank martinis and made love on the picnic table.

But most of the time he never made it home for dinner. His theater work kept him away and consumed. He'd ar-

rive home late at night and be up and gone before I awoke.
One morning I found a note he'd written the previous night,
his way of patting me on the head for being so devoted.

> I sit here, now at 11:00, having found no space on the
> 10:10 ferry, which left at 10:30, and blowing softly on
> the radio is Harry James, and for a moment I see us
> together, in a semidarkness, sensual together, and then I
> see us talking quietly and eating oysters. And then the
> moment, like the song, is over. There have been few
> moments between us lately, Elly, though I hope you
> know the truth that is in my heart, softly, evenly, lov-
> ing you.

Alone, waiting for him to come back to the island, I
would try to read one of my textbooks on sustainability or
natural resource conflict management. But I usually ended up
staring out the window toward the water, or walking down the
steep path from the house to the small patch of beach below
us. The cat always followed me. Maybe she thought another
flounder might come her way. On a blanket in the Northwest's
late-evening sunshine I would write letters to my friends who
were far away. Mostly, I'd write to Ginny, my almost love.

Ginny lived in Rhode Island, where I used to live. I met her
on a Tuesday night. The couple in apartment 5 was going at
it again.

"Why didn't you sweep the fucking floor? How fucking hard is it to sweep the fucking floor?" he'd yell in his insane high-pitched whine like some half-man, half-dying animal.

She, as usual, mumbled something apologetic and then I heard the tips of a broom skimming across vinyl flooring.

I put up with the fighting because I loved my three-room apartment in the small red brick building. It had a bay window seat that looked out over Thayer Street, the main drag running through campus. The seat was covered with multicolored woolen blankets that I bought in Mexico and shipped in my trunk all the way from California. The blankets, cheap and colorful as they were, set me a bit outside the New England prep school norm that surrounded me. I liked that. I liked sitting on them, my back against the edge where glass met wall, watching the world one floor below me. My legs sat long and straight on top of the scratchy material. After an hour of reading environmental policy reports, I'd put the yellow-highlighted pages down, stand, and stretch. The backs of my legs always looked sunburned.

I opened the door this time because after the sweeping stopped, the screaming began again.

"Would it kill you to have dinner ready on time? I work all day in that fucking cafeteria. What do you do? Huh? What do you do?"

"I work too," she tried.

He laughed an evil laugh. "You work? Taking care of

rich people's children is not working." He laughed again. "You are fucking pathetic."

He went into the other room, the one farthest away from my apartment, and turned on the television full volume. I could hear pots and pans being moved around the kitchen.

I walked out into the hallway and looked at their door, not sure what to do. I heard a noise behind me.

"They're at it again, huh?" a young woman said, coming down the stairs. "I feel so bad for her sometimes. Are they not answering?"

I was glad for the company in the darkened hallway. "No." I shifted my feet. "I haven't actually knocked on the door."

"Allow me," she said, and banged her fist on the door before I could say anything. The door opened and there stood a short pudgy moustached guy, about twenty-five. His beloved, a short and overweight girl with blonde curly hair and a down-turned mouth, was leaning against the kitchen sink behind him.

"Can I help you?" he growled at us.

The young woman smiled. "Listen, Matt. We'd like it if you could perhaps keep your fighting down to a whisper. I can hear you all the way upstairs. Again." We stared past him at the girl who was looking down at her feet, embarrassed.

"How are you doing, Kelly? You okay?" she asked her.

Kelly looked up and was about to say something, but Matt cut her short. "Yeah, sure. Sorry," he said, and slammed the door.

I was stunned. "Think we should call the police? Isn't that domestic violence?" I asked her.

"Nah. He's all talk. He'd never hurt her. He's just pissed off at the world. Give them another hour; they'll be having sex and making up."

I silently wondered why I'd never heard that part of the fighting.

"I've talked to her," she continued, "and believe it or not, she really loves him. I'm Virginia Wells. Ginny. Number nine."

"Yeah, I've seen you around," I said. "Elly Fisher. Number six," I said, pointing at my opened door.

"You go to Brown?" she asked.

"Yeah, I'm a grad student in the Environmental Studies department. You?"

She shook her head and some of the thin blonde hair that had been haphazardly locked into a red barrette came loose. "Nah. The design school."

"Cool," was all I could say. She was so tall and aristocratic-looking. She looked a lot like Princess Diana.

"Listen, I gotta get back upstairs. You want to get together? Do something next week, maybe? Lunch?"

Oh yeah. I didn't really care what I did with her. "Sure. You bet."

. . .

She left me a note taped to my door on Tuesday: "If you can, meet me at Louis' tomorrow at 1:00. I'll be there anyway. G."

I cut my Risk Assessment class and met Ginny at Louis' Restaurant. Short sweaty Louis himself served us our grilled cheese sandwiches with fries. We sat at the corner table and talked about school and our families and boys who kiss with their eyes closed. We shared a cigarette with our fifth cup of weak coffee, served in scratched white mugs.

She offered to pay when the check arrived.

"That's nice of you, Ginny, but it's only like four bucks," I said. "Let's just split it."

Ginny shrugged. "I wanted to buy you lunch. I did ask you out, you know."

The caffeine ricocheted around my chest like the road-runner in the cartoon. "Yes, you did ask me," I granted. "Was this, like, a date?"

"Maybe." Ginny grinned and threw down a twenty. "Let's go. I want you to see my show."

I glanced at the twenty on the table, grabbed my down coat and fleece hat, and raced after her. We walked side by side in the cold January day. I could tell people were looking at us, two attractive healthy young women bouncing with each step.

The wind whipped my hair against my face. "That's one thing I hate about that place," I said. "My hair is going to smell like a hamburger the rest of the day."

"Here. Let me smell," Ginny said. She stopped walking, wrapped her arm around my shoulder, and stuffed her face into my hair. Over her shoulder I could smell hers. It bore no resemblance to grease. "You're crazy," she said, laughing. "It smells great."

We went to one of the studios on the Rhode Island School of Design campus, where she proudly showed me her photography exhibit titled "Corners." It was cool and I said so. In each photograph the backdrop was the same corner; just two pink walls and a dark wooden floor, but in each picture a different person or thing was put in the corner. In one, a child sat on a tiny wooden chair facing the corner, his back to the camera. "Bad Child." In another, "The Circus Comes to Town," a clown stood, colorful red-nosed and slightly scary-looking with a smile that was more than a little evil. "An Unintentional Kiss" was a play on that popular black and white photo of a sailor kissing a nurse in Times Square after Japan surrendered. It was black and white as well, but no kissing; instead a large man in a sailor's uniform was backing a meek-looking woman in a nurse's uniform into the corner. You couldn't see either of their faces, but there was a menacing feel altogether.

I told Ginny my two favorites of the collection were "Push," which had a nude black man leaning forward against the two walls, his buttocks and arm and back muscles brightly lit and pulsing; and "Fruit," the most simple of the settings. A pine table filled in the 90-degree angle of the corner and on it was a brightly-colored basket of fruit. This was the only picture in which one of the walls of the corner was adorned with something, in this case a photograph of an older woman. It looked as if she could at any moment come to life and take a bite out of one of the pears.

"I'm really impressed," I said to Ginny on the walk home. The air had cooled considerably and I hugged my arms to my chest. "You shall be rich and famous one day, young lady."

"I'm already rich," Ginny countered. "And fame. Don't want it. Just want to keep taking pictures. Of everything. Because in pictures"—she stopped in front of our building and pushed her hand into her right front pocket of her tight jeans— "everything stays alive."

"How'd it go today?" I ask John as he pulls alongside me and gets out of the truck.

"Great," he says. "Do you mind coming in for a little while? We've got some time before the ferry leaves, and I have to make some calls."

The cat and I follow him in. I sit on the couch, grab an *Esquire*, and put my feet up on the coffee table. I listen to him talk to one of his stage managers. His new play opens in three weeks and he is already making sure everyone is where they need to be. He never even glances in my direction or offers me a drink.

Ginny phoned me two days later. "Come up. I want to show you something."

I combed my hair and ran upstairs.

Her small studio apartment was just as I had pictured it. There were photos and maps and album jackets thumbtacked to the walls, and clothing was piled up in every corner. There were dishes stacked in the sink. It smelled sweet and lived in. It felt like a Joni Mitchell song.

We listened to an ancient, scratched Bobby Sherman record while Ginny boiled water for tea in a beat-up aluminum pot. I sang along to "Easy Come, Easy Go," laughing because I knew every word by heart. She handed me a cup of Lipton tea and sat down beside me.

"Here. Look at this," she said as she leaned over and arranged some snapshots on the paint-splattered coffee table.

It was a collection of dog portraits mostly.

"They're dogs," I said, a little surprised by the tameness of her subject.

"Not just any dogs. My aunt Camilla's dogs. This is Aunt Camilla." Ginny handed me a photograph that showed a sad-faced woman with intelligent eyes. Her hair was short and she wore a man's fedora. She also had on a man's suit jacket and around her neck was a beautiful bolo tie made of brown and gold stone.

"No one in the family thinks much of her," Ginny said, frowning at the photograph. "She's marvelous and funny, but she's eccentric. Her strange habits make her an outsider, you know? She raises dogs. I think she has about sixty, mostly cocker spaniels."

"Is she a transvestite?"

"Sort of. She acts like a man. Or at least she dresses like one."

I wasn't certain if I should respond or not. I just watched her face.

"I don't think she cares about actually changing her sex. She isn't involved with anyone. Just her dogs. The family would disown her except she has a lot of money. Her husband died two years after they got married. And he was some huge industrialist. DuPont, I think."

"No way?" It was easy to be impressed by a name like that.

"Maybe it was something to do with steel. Or banking. I honestly don't know. But anyway, she lives over in Hopkinton on a huge estate and, well, she lives with her dogs. She's turning sixty-five this year. I thought it'd be a neat birthday present for her to have a couple of photos. What do you think?"

"They're beautiful."

The record stopped playing and Ginny looked at me. "I think I have a little bit of my aunt in me. I sometimes think I'd be better off as a man too." She leaned her head back on the couch and put her feet up. I liked the way her blonde hair, thin and long, swept across her shoulders. I wondered how someone so beautiful and feminine could want to be masculine, but I said nothing.

"Have you ever thought of being with a woman?" she suddenly asked without looking at me.

I pondered the question and thought it might be fun to play along, wishing to see what could become of being vague. "Sure, sometimes," I said. What I really wanted to know was if she wanted to be with me. I wanted her to like me, even to desire me. I remembered the baby powder I'd splashed across my chest and back that morning and wondered if she could smell it.

"I've never been with a woman, intimately I mean, but I think about it all the time. Not that I don't like men," Ginny admitted. "It's just that I've never had a good relationship with one. It's so much easier to be in the company of a woman."

I started to get a little nervous and picked up a photograph of a shiny cocker spaniel posing behind a red ball. "Yeah," I said, meaning it, "I know what you're saying." I liked being there with Ginny, my new pretty friend. Still, when it came right down to it, I knew there was no way I would—

She kissed me. On the lips. She leaned over, took my face in her left hand, and kissed my mouth. Hard. Then she pulled her head away and smiled.

"Want some more tea?" Ginny asked as she jumped up off the couch.

That Saturday, Ginny and I went to a concert at the Living Room, a local nightclub. I was standing in the midst of a huge pack of people swaying to the music, when a tall man with a blond ponytail trailing down his back bumped me. He was holding a tall sweaty glass of beer and smiling at me. He yelled something and I could vaguely make out, "I'm John!"

I yelled, "I'm Elly!" and then looked back at the stage. I felt his warmth next to me more strongly as the song went on, and to check him out I pretended to be looking for someone past his shoulders. I caught his eye for a second but my vision jerked over to where Ginny was standing, talking to a group of girls. Perched next to a thick wood beam holding the room up, she was laughing, her hair floating out from her head and catching the outskirts of the spotlights. For a moment I was stunned with jealousy.

I dated John, who turned out to be an actor. His smiles always seemed touched by melancholy. There was an intense brooding side to his laughter and I was drawn into his struggles, emotional and professional. It was easy to neglect myself and look after him.

I had given him my phone number the night of the concert, and he asked me to go with him to see the Boston Symphony the following Friday. I started coughing Wednesday and sneezed and slept through Thursday. Friday morning I phoned him to apologize.

"My mother warned me about listening to symphony music under the influence of a fever," I kidded him. He laughed, and I knew he was disappointed, which I was glad about.

On Friday night there was a knock at my door. John stood on the threshold, smiling. "It's our first date. How can we let a little cold spoil it?"

I had no energy to feel embarrassed. I was wearing a pair of gray sweatpants with holes in the knees, a ratty old blue sweater, and two different socks.

"Come in," I said.

He was carrying a crumpled paper bag. "What's in there?" I asked.

"Some tea. Sit back down. I'm here to help."

I did as I was told and he covered my lap with one of the Mexican blankets I had yanked off the window seat and dragged across the dusty floor. I wiped my nose, closed my eyes, and let him find his way around my kitchen. A few minutes later I took the mug of tea he handed me as he slid down onto the couch next to me, casually shoving aside a few hundred recently used tissues.

"Ready for the concert?" he asked. He pulled out a cassette tape from his bag. It was the Boston Symphony Orchestra playing Prokofiev, Strauss, and Brahms. He held my hand during the second side. I tried to blow my nose between movements.

When the tape ended, he got up, ejected it from the tape player, and put it in his back pocket. I felt well enough to notice how well his jeans fit his body. He had on a nice brown shirt too. Darn, he was cute.

He moved his face close to mine.

"What are you doing? Are you crazy?" I said through my stuffed nose.

He smirked. "What can I say? My mother never warned me about kissing a beautiful girl with a runny nose."

"I'm glad you met a nice guy," Ginny said when I told her a couple of weeks later about John and our first date, but I could tell she was pissed off. I didn't blame her. Since that first kiss we had hardly spent any time together. She was working on some new antiquing technique and I was working on getting through graduate school and making John fall in love with me.

I wanted to keep Ginny interested in me. Out of vanity.

Or just in case things didn't mesh with John. In March I invited her over to play dress-up and watch the Academy Awards.

That night I wore an Asian kimono I'd bought in a downtown Providence thrift store. I put my hair up and clipped it into a gaudy butterfly clip. Ginny showed up in a black velvet minidress, with a rhinestone choker around her neck, carrying a jeweled cigarette holder.

"Dahling," she said as she air-kissed me and sauntered into my living room.

I handed her a martini glass filled with peppermint schnapps.

"To us," Ginny toasted. "Gorgeous women that we are."

"To us," I replied. We both downed the schnapps and I refilled our glasses.

While sitting on the couch in John's house on Bainbridge Island I pick at a hangnail and watch the cat lick her butt with her back paw stuck straight up in the air to make way for her head. A seagull flies by the deck and John picks up the phone. I wait for him to remember I'm in the room with him. I didn't use to do that. The first months we were together were exciting enough. He barely let me be in a room without him standing right by my side. I was his. Then he had been offered that great job in Seattle—running high school theater workshops all over western Washington. That, plus plenty of money available to produce two or three of his own shows a year. A dream job.

"Go with me."

"But I'm in graduate school. You know, where you spend a lot of money and buy a degree? I still have more classes to take before they let me get mine."

"Go with me," he had repeated. "I can't do this without you. You can always continue your studies at the University of Washington. I checked. They have an even better Environmental Studies department than this one."

"You checked?" I'd figured that meant he really loved me.

Ginny and I snuggled close on the couch and made fun of the sequined gowns and long-winded acceptance speeches. Our laughter mingled like we were sisters. When Carly Simon's "Let the River Run" won the award for best song, Ginny took my hand in hers. I looked at her and she leaned over and kissed me. I kissed her back, tasting the minty alcohol on her tongue. Her hand moved from the back of my neck and pushed into the slit in the front of my red and orange kimono. She barely grazed my left breast when I drew back. The tension hit us like a piano thrown from a high roof.

"What do you want from me?" Ginny asked, an angry pout on her face. "I kind of got the feeling this was going somewhere."

I moved against the sharp wooden arm of the couch, its hard corner dug into my lower back. "I am attracted to you, Ginny, but I want to see where things go with John." I swallowed hard and looked out the kitchen window, at the television set, the floor, my hands. "I didn't mean to tease you. I just don't, I don't know, I think I'm more straight than I thought I was. And besides . . ."

"Besides, what?" Ginny said, getting up.

"John asked me to go with him to Seattle. I'm gonna go with him."

"What? You're kidding, right? You just met him. You barely know him. And you're going to drop out of school and follow him like some loser chick? Like that girl who lives next door and gets yelled at?"

As much as her accusation stung, I knew she was right. I was willing to follow John. It didn't matter to me. It was easier this way. Easier because I was falling in love with Ginny.

I moved closer to her and uttered what I imagined would be like a salve on a cat scratch. "I want to be friends. Good friends. I adore you. I think you're incredibly beautiful and talented and I can't imagine letting you disappear from my life just because we don't have sex."

She sighed and let her head fall back. I hugged her. I burrowed my face into her soft sweet hair and I kept my palms flat on her back for a long time, as I pulled her into me. Then I let go.

• • •

Ginny went with me to see John's final production for Trinity Rep Conservatory. He'd written the piece, which was called *The Man In White*. In it he portrayed two dozen characters from plays and movies and stories and fables, all seamlessly woven into one dialogue. It was very good, and I realized with some anticipation that he was going to be a great success in Seattle.

After the performance I introduced John to Ginny. He knew very little about our friendship except that we hung out together when he and I were apart. He knew I was leaving with him; that's what mattered.

I watched the two of them standing next to each other on the sidewalk; both tall and thin and blond, they could have been siblings.

"You were great. Really," Ginny said to John. "Elly told me you were good, but this was more than good."

John shifted his weight to one foot and tucked his hands into the front pockets of his jeans. I loved him when he stood like that, like an eleven-year-old. "You take photographs, right?"

"Art," I said quickly. "Not just pictures. Art." I looked at Ginny. "John has never seen your work. Maybe we should get together before we leave and you can show him your stuff."

"Yeah. Sure," Ginny replied, and smiled the way I'd seen her smile at a fellow art student who was criticizing her work at an exhibition without knowing Ginny was the artist. Just a slight line across her face.

We invited Ginny to come out for a late supper with us.

"Nope. Thanks anyway. Gotta go do things."

She wandered away, thin strands of her hair sticking out under a blue and white striped wool cap.

The ferry back to Seattle will sail without me if we don't leave, but John is still on the telephone, so I don't bother him.

"Let's go," John says as he hangs up and looks at the clock on the wall. "You'll just make it."

I grab my pack and throw it into the back of the truck. I blow a kiss to Little Ricky and we back out of the driveway. John plays a Pat Metheny tape during the drive to the ferry dock.

"Hey, thanks for this," I say.

"Least I can do."

I am taken aback. Is he aware of my loss, I wonder. "What do you mean?"

"You know, what with leaving school and now you're not really doing what you set out to do. And well, I know it's because of me. I know what you did because of me. What you gave up. And I'm sorry you're not happy."

"Why do you think I'm not happy?" I am relieved when I see that the ferry is already docked and loading cars.

"Because I know how much you look forward to spend-ing a day with a cat that doesn't give a shit about you one way or another."

In June, right before I moved to the Northwest with John, there was a knock on my door. I greeted a corpulent man with a gray beard that looked like wainscoting clumsily glued to his pouchy cheeks.

"Fester Reingold, private detective. You must be Vir-ginia Wells," he said in a gravelly voice, one he got from either smoking too much or from watching too many Bogart films.

"Ginny lives in number nine. Easy mistake to make," I said, glancing at the number six on my door. "Come on, I'll show you where it is," I told him, walking in front of him up the stairs, before he could protest. I knocked on Ginny's door, a black and white photograph of the number nine glued over the actual number. She didn't look surprised to see the man, a sloppy Burl Ives imitation, hovering there.

"Fester Reingold, private detective. You must be Vir-ginia Wells," he repeated. I looked at Ginny and noticed the strain on her face. "What's going on, Ginny?" I asked.

"Come in, Mr. Reingold." Ginny gestured to the couch behind her. As he walked past her and stood in her living room taking up more space than her coffee table, she leaned into me and whispered, "It's Aunt Camilla. No one can find her."

"What?"

"Everyone else seems to think she's gone off to one of her dog shows or something, but she never called to say good-bye to me and she's been gone for almost three weeks now. She'd never leave for so long without telling me first."

"Have you called the police? Why hire this guy?" I asked, while watching him make himself comfortable on her couch.

"I did, but they didn't think there was anything sus-picious going on. William, her secretary, knows her pretty well and he believes she's in Europe. Look, I've got to talk to this guy. Let me call you later," she said, and shut the door on me.

It is cold and windy during the ride back to Seattle, so I buy a cup of coffee and slide across a beige vinyl seat at the rear of the boat. I stare out the window and catch a glimpse of Mount Rainier between swiftly moving clouds. The sky and the water are a steel-colored gray. I think about John and Seattle and the cat and I start to cry. A group of Japanese tourists sits down across from me. I wipe my face and watch the seagulls fly among the waves.

Aunt Camilla's skeleton was found in the septic tank on her property a year and a half after she disappeared. Police suspect her private secretary, William Ryan, of murdering her, but have not yet found enough evidence to prove it. When I said good-bye to Ginny in her apartment that summer, she was stirring a pot of soup on her stove. I hugged her and told her to take good care. I blew her a kiss before I closed the door of apartment nine.

I am glad to be home, off the island, in my tiny apartment above a Greek pizzeria. George, the slumped-over and greasy-faced owner, tells everyone who walks through the door that he invented feta and spinach pizza. I eat one of those inventions every Thursday night, discounted because George doesn't have to charge me for a take-out box. I bring my own platter downstairs, warm from my oven, after George calls me to tell me my pie is ready.

Craps

ELLY: A WONDERFUL man has fallen in love with me and I can't find it in me to fall in love back. And I really want to.

Maxine: Why?

Elly: Well, because of the checklist, you know? He's got almost all the traits I want in a man. He's good-looking and strong and funny and caring and sensitive and he idolizes me and we have a lot of fun together. Plus, sex is very, very good.

Maxine: So where's the problem?

Elly: Well, he's stupid. Not stupid. That's mean. He's just . . . Well, he just doesn't live up to my intellectual expectations. He's a nice Catholic boy. He went to a Catholic high school and Catholic college. He thinks abortion is bad because the Pope says so. I don't know, he's just kind of naive, dumb. Maybe young is a better word.

Maxine: Do you mind me asking what his name is?

Elly: Why would I mind? Neilson. Neil. I like that name. It's playful.

Maxine: Let's get back to what you just said about Neil being less intelligent than you'd like him to be. Can you give me an example?

Elly: Well, a few weeks ago we were watching this Italian movie and it was dealing with Marxism, and at the end of it he turned to me and asked, "How did Marxism get to Italy?" And I thought, that's not a stupid question. I can deal with curiosity. So I start explaining about how maybe people were reading Karl Marx's books and tracts and starting small groups to talk about it. And more people started reading the works, and more people listened to other people speaking, and the books and the ideas eventually spread to Italy. I said it was a natural progression of ideas.

Maxine: And?

Elly: He said, "But who was the person who actually brought the idea of Marxism to Italy?" Like he didn't get it at all, that ideas are living things, not these static tree branches that someone has to actually carry from one place to another. We both got really frustrated. And so I said, "How did Christianity spread around Europe?" thinking this would give him more perspective. But he just sort of shrugged a shoulder and said, "The disciples spread the word of Jesus." And I said, "So, you think that it was these twelve guys wandering around the planet who got the whole world to believe in Jesus?" And he just looked at me, blankly. I think he wanted to say yes, but thought better of it. It's like he can't think and hold a conversation at the same time. I could tell I was making him miserable.

Maxine: And?

Elly: And. I told him he should probably leave.

Maxine: What did that accomplish?

Elly: I didn't have to see him the rest of the night. I mean, he only eats pizza and hot dogs for dinner.

Maxine: You take issue with his diet too?

Elly: No. I couldn't care less what he eats. I take that back. I do care what he eats in that I care that he has choices, and should be aware of them, but he's not. He doesn't take advantage of what's out there. He only knows what he knows.

Maxine: Who are you referring to?

Elly: What do you mean?

Maxine: I am asking whether you are really referring to yourself in that last statement. The one where you say Neil should take advantage of what's out there.

Elly: I'm referring to him. Me. Both of us, I guess. Him for some things. Me for others. I suppose I'm no different that way. Not seeing all my choices. Not choosing to see all my choices. Sometimes I feel like a goldfish in a glass bowl, swimming in circles, waiting for my owner to drop some food on my head.

Maxine: Why?

Elly: Because I know it's the easy way to be. It's easier to just float and wait, float and wait. But it's not the way I want to be.

Maxine: How do you want to be?

Elly: I want to be able to take more initiative without thinking about the outcomes before they even happen. Weren't we talking about Neil and his predilection for hot dogs?

Maxine: You've continued to see him?

Elly: Sure. I mean, he's my best friend right now. He helped me get through my breakup with John. That was hard.

Maxine: Do you want to talk about John?

Elly: No. We had a good time. Thing is, he's still having a good time, and I'm not. It's just that I hate the idea of losing a friend like that.

Maxine: Friends are important.

Elly: Sure. I go out of my way to try to convince ex-lovers to stay in my life, even if they've broken up with me. That's weird, huh?

Maxine: You think it's weird to want to hang on to people who've made you happy?

Elly: No, I guess not. Maybe just greedy.

Maxine: Let's get back to Neil. What are some of the characteristics, other than his ignorance, that you find difficult to be with?

Elly: His thoughtlessness. Clumsiness. Okay, a few weeks ago he sent me this bouquet of flowers and on the note he wrote something like, "The smell of these flowers cannot compare to your beautiful fragrance." And he spelled the word *fragrance* wrong. I got so mad, I threw out the flowers.

Maxine: You were mad about the spelling error or was it something else?

Elly: What?

Maxine: He misspelled a word and you got angry at him. Maybe the misspelling set off something else that made you mad.

Elly: You've lost me.

Maxine: What I mean to say is there may be a subconscious dilemma having to do with becoming mad when someone you love makes a mistake. Or doesn't do the right thing, in other words.

Elly: No, I think it's just that I hate imperfection. Period.

Maxine: In others as well as yourself?

Elly: More so in myself. I'm very self-critical.

Maxine: But it's easier to judge the actions of others than it is to judge yourself?

Elly: No kidding. It's always easier to spot other people's foibles. I'd rather ignore my own if I can. Maybe that's why I'm here. I'd like to be able to face my insecurities head-on, learn some strategies for making my way without finding blame in everything and everyone. I know Neil is not the right guy for me, but it's easy to have him around to blame my unhappiness on. Does that make sense?

Maxine: Very much so. You're uncertain about more than one

part of your life. Which part is it that you think stands out from the others?

Elly: How much more time do we have?

Maxine: Let's not concern ourselves with time.

Elly: My professional life, for one. My goals. I mean, I've gone to college and graduate school and I still don't know what's next. At what point do I stop wondering what I want to be when I grow up?

Maxine: I should hope you never stop wondering what to do next. Did you earn a Ph.D.?

Elly: Do pigs fly? Nope. I dropped out before finishing my M.A.

Maxine: What do you do for a living?

Elly: I'm an intern at Seattle City Light.

Maxine: Doing what?

Elly: Conservation outreach.

Maxine: Can you be more specific?

Elly: I work on the Zoo-Doo project.

Maxine: And that is?

Elly: Using zoo animal shit for composting in public gardens. Can we move on?

Maxine: Sure. You brought up your professional concerns.

Elly: I know. I just can't talk about this right now. My job is my job. I'll be at a different one next month, or the month after that. This is short term.

Maxine: What would you like to move on to doing?

Elly: What I'd like to move on to is another subject altogether. I'm sorry, was that rude?

Maxine: Not in the least. We can come back to it. What other part of your life causes you worry?

Elly: Men. For some demented reason I think I can't enjoy my life unless I have a man in it, even though I know that's not true. I should be able to handle being alone, but I turn from one man to the next, usually without being very discriminating. After a while it gets old. Not always. But you know what I mean . . . it gets stale. But I hang on. The guy hangs on. And I turn on them for hanging on.

Maxine: Can you elaborate on that?

Elly: I turn into a bitch. In the long run my respect for men who stay with a woman who is not nice goes way down. I tell them they're all wrong for me, but that just seems to get them more committed. Like here. Here's a letter from Neil that he wrote after the fragrance episode. I spent weeks trying to convince him that he shouldn't love me and he writes me this apologetic letter. Do you want to read it or should I?

Maxine: Go ahead.

Elly: "Dear Elly, I found starting this letter a paralyzing enterprise. I am scared to say something wrong, or use the wrong punctuation. I know it would be the last straw. I'm writing this letter to prove that I am literate and not lacking in depth of knowledge, thought, feeling, or ability to absorb new ideas. Intelligence, in my opinion, is obtained from experiencing

something or someone. Life is short, and in my lifetime I will experience many things, but not everything the world has to offer. I invite these experiences, whatever they may be, and feel nourished by the time I go to sleep, and hungry for more by the time I wake up. However long I'm blessed with life on this planet, I will look forward to every sunrise and sunset, and the time in between. I would like to spend the rest of my sunrises and sunsets and the time in between with you, although I know deep down that this dream will not come true. My love for you is infinite, ferocious, deafening, electric, blinding, intense . . . I could go on forever creating words to express my feelings for you. I love you, Neilson." Am I a shit or what? I mean, the guy is trying like hell and I give him grief over the littlest things.

Maxine: Any spelling errors in this one?

Elly: Yeah. A few. But I overlooked them when I read it so I wouldn't get mad at him. Why can't I just love him? Simply and totally?

Maxine: Is that what you want, to love someone simply and totally?

Elly: Actually, now that you mention it, it is what I want. But I don't know if I'm capable of that. Nothing is simple any-more. It's hard to be unconditional, to just like someone for who they are. At least in my mind. I mean, it's like I'm playing chess all the time, even in relationships, trying to think as many moves ahead as I can so that I can win.

Maxine: What do you win?

Elly: I don't know. I get to be in control. I get to make the decisions. That way if things go badly, I can blame myself, even if outwardly I pretend to blame the other person.

Maxine: Why blame? Why not take credit for making sound decisions? Haven't there been accomplishments in your life?

Elly: Not enough. Especially the school thing. I was the one in the family who was going to succeed, make everyone proud, live up to their expectations. My getting into a good school was a big coup for my father. He and Mom never went to college, and here I was going to graduate school.

Maxine: What's your dad do?

Elly: Contractor. He builds developments in southern California. He's like the anti-Christ to me.

Maxine: How is that to deal with?

Elly: We don't talk about it. He knows what I do. I know what he does. Never the twain shall meet. But it wasn't always like that.

Maxine: You had a good relationship with your father growing up?

Elly: I would have done anything to please him. I'd beg him to let me hold the level while he screwed something in. I felt like a princess if he let me bring him his water on a job. I loved being his center of attention. I'm still that way with men. I sometimes do anything to get them to notice me. Hold the ladder straight. Dance a little dance to please them.

Maxine: Were you sexually abused as a child?

Elly: No. Nothing ever happened to me. I had a safe wonderful childhood filled with the sounds of Muzak coming in over the intercom system my dad installed all over the house. No weird uncles or stepbrothers raping me in the night, thank you very much.

Maxine: Okay. Why don't you continue on the topic of living up to expectations?

Elly: You mean how it is I'm feeling like an utter failure right now? Dropping out of graduate school and breaking up with John just about yanked all my confidence. I think that's why I picked Neil. He's safe. No big investment. I can look to greater things and not have him hold me back. God, that's mean.

Maxine: No, it's honest. If you really don't see that the relationship is worth fighting for—

Elly: But I am here fighting for it, aren't I?

Maxine: I'm not sure exactly what you're fighting for. I don't think you're sure either.

Elly: It's all pretty scary, you know, trying to figure this out. Everything is all mishmashed together.

Maxine: What scares you the most right now?

Elly: I'm feeling somewhat paranoid about my future, that it's going to turn out to be a particularly lonely one. You know, it's funny I said paranoid. On the way here today I was riding the bus and this guy wearing a medical coat got on and sat next to me. Being a hopeless flirt, I notice that he's in the medical profession and immediately began fantasizing about being married to a doctor and thinking how much fun it would be to tell our kids we met on a bus. I turned and asked him what kind of doctor he is. He said he was a third-year resident in psychiatry. He had a nice smile and he seemed interested, so I asked him what he'd done today. He said he'd just come from a group therapy session with a bunch of paranoid adults. Being the wit that I am, I said, "Were they talking about me?"

Maxine: That's funny. Did he laugh?

Elly: Yes, it is, thank you very much. He looked at me with a totally quizzical expression and asked, "Why would they be talking about you?" The perfect guy is never going to come out of the woodwork.

Maxine: I don't believe you really believe that. Now, back to what we were discussing. What do you see as a short-term goal?

Elly: Quit the job I'm doing, use my skills more, meet Mr. Perfect, see the world.

Maxine: All in the next year?

Elly: Why not? I don't want to die bored. Now, that's one of my biggest obstacles if you really want to know: fear of dying before I accomplish great things.

Maxine: What do you think would happen if you died without accomplishing great things?

Elly: I'd be a dead anonymous person, which freaks me out. I want to leave my name on something important. Peering out for all the world to see. Do you think this makes me a complete egomaniac, or what?

Maxine: Why don't you not worry so much what kind of impression you make on me.

Elly: But I'm paying you to make an impression of me, no?

Maxine: Let's get back to your father. How have his opinions of you changed the way you view yourself?

Elly: I come here to talk about Neilson and you keep pushing me to talk about my father. Are you a Freudian?

Maxine: I'm just me, Elly. I think it would be helpful for you to sift through your past relationships a little before we try to deal with Neilson. Are you uncomfortable with that?

Elly: Am I uncomfortable talking about the man who would be king?

Maxine: Your father?

Elly: No, Sean Connery. Of course I'm referring to my father. It's the pressure thing. My grandmother died a couple of years ago and we were all at my aunt's house after the funeral and my dad says to no one in particular, "I'll never die. I'll be in the grave and my daughter will stand on top of it and scream, 'Get up, Dad,' and I'll rise up." Hello? Is that sick or what? You know, he once bet me in Las Vegas. I was four years old and he was playing craps and Mom and I walked by the table and he grabbed me and put me right on the edge of it and said, "I'm betting my daughter." Swear to God. All the players and dealers were laughing and I was scared out of my mind. So he rolled the dice and after they hit the opposite wall, the dealer yelled, "Craps, you lose." My father handed me over to one of the men and he walked away with me, and I remember screaming bloody murder and they all just stood around laughing. What do you think that did to me?

Maxine: Probably a pretty traumatic thing for a four-year-old to experience. But I bet you forgave him.

Elly: Sure, I've forgiven him for everything rotten he's ever done. I'm good at forgiveness, even if I do hold grudges forever. I'd really rather not keep talking about him.

Maxine: Okay. We can talk about something else next time. Let's go out to the front desk and schedule our next session, shall we?

Other Fish *in the* Sea

ELLY awakens and moves her right hand across her eyes. She is awake, yet still asleep. She pulls on the gray sweatpants she finds still lying on the floor, tries to unknot the white string, but finally gives up and lets the pants sag around her jutting hips. She yanks a white cotton turtleneck over the Cousteau Society T-shirt she slept in and goes out the front door of her tiny Capitol Hill apartment, hugging a blue binder to her chest. The distant Seattle skyline is a winter gray, like a permanently rain-streaked window. She walks slowly down Olive Street to the Krazy Kat Kafe three blocks away, orders a double cappuccino from Owen, a young guy with a silver cross dangling from his left ear, and takes it to a wobbly wooden table near the back. As she sips the hot coffee, Elly is aware of a lingering dizziness from the cold medicine she took before going to bed. She is not awake, but not asleep, not connected to the painted green chair on which she sits. A young couple, dressed in black, walks in the front door. In the background Louis Armstrong sings a song about standing on a corner. As Elly looks down at the unfinished reports on sewer runoff she needs to turn in to the Water Quality Coalition, her head begins to spin and she watches her right hand, in slow motion, bring the yellow mug down to the table. She is glad she does not burn herself with the white foam. It is her last thought.

Elly awakens in a room, a white room. Her head feels like a rock. She knows, but does not know why she knows, that other people are in the room with her. There is a soft hum, but not from the lights above her. It is all she hears. She cannot even hear the sound of her own breathing, cannot feel her chest rise and fall, but she senses she is being squeezed together. A man's voice speaks. One ear hears him. The other searches out the hum, the constant hum. The voice tells her that she will be going on a trip, traveling. Somewhere. Elly tries to push the words into her thoughts, but they lie flat on her forehead, not connected to meaning. She tries to move her hand to wipe them into her eyes and onto her brain, but she cannot move her right hand because now it is humming. Her whole body is humming. She does not know if her eyes are open or closed. There is white everywhere.

· · ·

Elly awoke to the sounds of surf and seagulls and cars and children's laughter and a radio playing music somewhere close by. She was standing on a beach with other people, some of them smiling. Others crying. Two or three were talking frantically, but she could not understand the words. Slowly the air found its way into her nose and she breathed deeply and listened.

"Did anyone see *The Manchurian Candidate*?" an older man, maybe in his fifties, asked the group. "I think this is a collective brainwash."

"I'm afraid," said a redheaded woman. She looked around to see if someone else was afraid too.

"Where are we?" asked another. A woman.

"Is this another time?"

"Why us?"

"Are we dead?"

"Do we wish we were dead?"

"I say we check out where we are," said a handsome young woman with dark hair and dark eyes.

Everyone nodded, including Elly. They looked around them for some sign of content, reality. Children played in the sand, like children anywhere. The sun was high and the wind felt warm on Elly's face. The gulls flew overhead without paying them heed. A few families with children were running in and out of the surf. Elly caught the eye of a young woman in an old-fashioned bathing suit. She watched as the mother called her child's name, Mindy, aloud, and ordered her back to the woolen, stained blanket. Then the mother turned her gaze away from the group.

Elly moved next to the dark-haired woman. She was Elly's age, thirty, or maybe a year or two older, and Elly felt oddly comforted by being beside her. A gust of wind blew and one of the men in the group yelped, and his right hand covered his mouth like the teenager in a horror movie who discovers his girlfriend's mutilated body in the basement.

"What is it?" another man, short and balding, asked.

"Look at this," the man said, pointing at a page of a newspaper blown from across the beach.

The date on the top of the paper read "July 18, 1942."

They sat in a circle behind a dune, away from the families on the beach. They looked at one another, searching one another's eyes for answers. Eleven of them sat there, dressed all in white; long, sleeveless linen dresses on the five women, and cotton trousers and T-shirts on the six men. The dark-haired woman spoke up again.

"I just don't get it. Why send us here with no explanation? You guys have pockets in your pants, don't you? Check and see if there's something in them."

The soft rustle of skin on cloth settled for a moment on the air.

A man with a ruddy complexion and frizzy long hair pulled a scrap of paper from his pocket and raised it above his head.

"I found something. I found a slip of paper!" he screamed.

"Open it. Read it, for God's sake."

He unfolded a piece of white lined notebook paper, or maybe computer paper. Elly thought she saw a trace of green on the paper's border.

Welcome to 1942. Do not panic. No harm will come to you. If you feel as if you are dreaming, you are. If the world beneath you feels hard and real, it is. Do not spend your short time asking for answers. You have been given a moment of time. Do with it as you wish. There is a train station ½ mile south of here. At exactly 6:15 p.m. a train will be waiting at the station. You must be on it. You must be on it.

Someone began to cry softly and Elly considered comforting the woman, but her mind wandered too quickly. What to think? What to do? The paper said there were no answers. Okay, so maybe this was a dream. That was okay. She'd had some strange dreams before, the kind that stayed with her for a day or so and made her feel as if she never quite woke up from them. Like the one where her mother called and told her that Elly's father had died from pancreatic cancer. She woke up crying and believed he was actually gone for almost a whole day.

The dark-haired woman's voice broke the panic that paralyzed the group. "Well, I don't know about the rest of you, but I'm going with the dream theory, and as long as we've only got a couple of nanoseconds to enjoy this dream, let's get to it. I haven't had a swim in the ocean in years."

"You got that right, babe." Elly smiled at her own burst of excitement, and pulled the woman up with her and they started off together down the beach toward the small shops. The crying woman and the other two women stood up and chased after them.

Now they were five.

The redhead with tear-streaked cheeks started first. "So girls, I'm from Arizona and I sell real estate. My name is—"

"Stop!" yelled the dark-haired woman. "I don't want to know who you are or where you came from. This is probably a dream, so you're just a mix of all those subconscious collections of people in my life, anyway. Let's leave the past in the past for the day, okay? I mean, this is so fucking weird that I can't even begin to fathom what's happening here, let alone make small talk."

"That's fine with me," the redhead conceded. "I just thought if we were going to spend the next . . . who has a watch? Oh my God. If no one has a watch, how are we going to know when six fifteen is? We have to be on that train, girls. Remember? We must be on that train."

"I don't think any of us will miss that train, my dear friend. So why don't you stop whining and start enjoying the 1940s. So, where are all the boys?" asked a tall blonde woman of about forty.

All but the red-haired woman laughed.

"I do believe there's a war on, if it really is 1942. I would guess most of the boys are over in Europe killing Germans," said the fifth woman, a slight Amerasian with a deep dimple in her left cheek.

"Oh shit, you're right. Why the hell would whoever sent us here send us back in the middle of a war?" asked the dark-haired woman.

Dream or no dream, Elly had to say it. "Do you think maybe we're here for some purpose? Maybe we're supposed to do something about the war. Like stop the Hiroshima bombing. Or kill Hitler, even?"

They had reached the edge of the beach, where the few businesses in the tiny town had set up shop. The surf was light, but the salt of a crashing wave sprayed them. The dark-haired woman crossed her arms and grinned. "You and what army? How do you plan on going over to Germany, killing Adolf, and getting back in time to catch a very mysterious train back home?"

"No! Absolutely not!" the blonde woman screamed in frustration. "We are not here to do anything but enjoy the moment. Remember? The moment of time we were given is like a gift. No, not *like* a gift. It is a gift. We're not to do anything with it but take it, watch it, lap it up like some thirsty dog at a curb where some moron left his sprinkler running too long because he's inside watching a football game. We aren't here to intervene. We're just here to watch." She looked up toward the blue sky and said, "Why on earth did you put me in a cool dream like this with a bunch of politically correct nineties women?"

Elly laughed at the woman's rants, and even though she could not help thinking there was a purpose to their visit—that was what her mother had taught her; that nothing just happens—she did want to swim in the ocean and maybe talk to the people on the beach. This was a moment for them to welcome. All eleven of them, in any way they chose. A flash. A sip of cool sweet tea on a humid day; a hug from a lover when you first awake. No, this was an okay thing. No more questions. No more fears. Just the moment.

Five women in white linen dresses and bare feet entered the small ramshackle beach shop next to The Tides Motel. On the shelves and hanging on hooks were flowered rubber bathing caps, bathing suits, large pink towels, Coca-Cola in a bottle, Kodak film, candy that none of the women remembered ever seeing before. Playing cards, cigarettes, bright red plastic pails and shovels.

"Wait," said the redhead, while holding a swanky blue and white polka-dotted bathing suit against her body. "We have no money."

"If this is a dream," said the blonde woman, "then we don't need to wear bathing suits."

"But if it isn't a dream, and we get arrested for nude swimming, then we might end up in jail. And I don't know about you, but I don't think I want to be hanging out in a jail cell at six fifteen tonight," said the red-haired woman, her arms stiffly on her hips.

"Point well taken," agreed the dark-haired woman. "Not that I really believe this could be happening, but just to be safe, let's just go find a secluded spot and swim to our heart's content."

Elly liked this woman and was glad to have her along in her dream. For an instant she wondered if she were the subconscious person she always wished she could be: defiant and decisive. God, how she longed to trust herself the way she trusted this stranger beside her. Maybe all these people were just a collection of the personalities that have come and gone in her life. Was the red-haired woman her fearful self? The one that, as a new graduate student in the Environmental Studies program at the University of Washington, drank Pepto-Bismol for a week, and almost passed out the first time she had to teach a seminar? What about the men? How did they fit into her subconscious?

"Boy, no wonder I got some evil eyes from the beach people. I just realized I should be one of those innocent Japanese locked up in a detention camp right now," the Asian woman sighed. "As long as I'm free, I'm going antique shopping."

"What? What antiques?" asked the blonde.

"Do you have any idea what one of those 1942 comic books is worth today? And what about old Coke bottles. I bet I can sort through people's trash and find hundreds of little treasures I can take back with me."

Laughing with disbelief, Elly said, "Are you crazy? Did you forget this is a dream? You're going to spend your dream scrounging around garbage cans?"

"Well, maybe, like everyone keeps subtly hinting at but nobody is willing to admit, this is not a dream. What if we're part of some kind of experiment, some government thing, and we were randomly chosen or something, and transported back, and—poo, I don't know. All I'm saying is the big *What if?* You know? And so what. If it's real, I get to take home all these forties things and prove to people I went back in time, and if not, well, what else is there to do? I'm not into swimming and, you know, I'll see you guys at the train." And she walked off.

Elly shrugged her shoulders, as did the dark-haired woman. They walked out of the shop and headed to the water, away from the dozen or so families sprawled like freckles across the plain sand. The red-haired woman said, "I changed my mind. I'm going to find the men."

"Speaking of men," giggled the blonde woman as she fluffed her hair and looked over to a group of soldiers drinking beer in the parking lot. Elly and the dark-haired woman watched as she approached the smiling men. For a second she glanced back over her shoulder and with her right hand waved a beauty-queen wave.

They swam together in the gentle surf like otters, laughing and splashing each other's naked bodies. Elly and the woman with dark hair emerged drenched from the ocean, put their white dresses on over their sticky bodies, and stretched out behind two grassy sand dunes.

"Ah, this is the life," Elly said, as she ran her fingers through her wet salty hair. "I haven't had a vacation in a long time." I guess you could count the obligatory trip last February to San Diego to see my folks, she thought. There was a reason she now lived in Seattle while all her relatives lived in southern

California. Too many opinions from too many people crowded her from the moment she disembarked from some Boeing jet. "Would it kill you to wear a dress?" "How hard could it be to get one master's degree?" "How can you stand all that rain?"

One day last summer she had convinced her cousin Jennifer to take a day off from work and they played together all day. Swam in the ocean, shared a steaming platter of fish tacos, drank two beers apiece. Hung out side by side just as Elly was doing now with a dark-haired stranger. She loved Jennifer; she was her favorite relative, in fact. But she was no more intimate with her, shared no more of her fears about loneliness and failure, than she did with anyone else in her life. Now she wanted to let herself go with the woman beside her, only she wasn't sure how.

"I'm happy for your rest and relaxation." The dark-haired woman paused and swept a dripping clump of hair from her forehead. "I just wonder how this is all going to play out."

Elly rolled onto her left forearm. "Play out? What do you mean? Please don't make me any more freaked out than I already am. I was just beginning to ignore the larger implications of this, this thing, and now you've slapped it back in my face. So much for remaining paranoid-free." She took a deep breath. Her stomach acid began churning. She swallowed loudly enough for the other woman to hear.

"Fine. Fine. Have it your way. The swim was great, don't get me wrong. But this is ridiculous, just sitting here like this. Look," she said, sitting up, determined to make her point. "I, for one, am not sure I really want to go back. I—"

"No," Elly interrupted. "Don't think about it or I will too." She heard the words, but they took even her by surprise.

The dark-haired woman smirked, her eyes narrowed. "Really? Your life is so bad back home that you'd consider leaving everything? Everyone you know?"

"I didn't say that." Elly closed her eyes tightly. The few small tears forming under the lids stayed hidden. "Yes, I did. I can't believe I said that. I have a perfectly fine life. A bit lonely, but fine. I mean, I have a great job and a few friends who I hang out with. . . ." God, why not just tell her everything? That she wakes and walks like a zombie to the same coffee place every day. Drinks a double cappuccino. Goes to work, smiles and chats with the dozen or so liberal-minded, hip urbanites she works with at the Water Quality Coalition. Saving our waterways one person at a time. For seven bucks an hour, Elly researches how human behavior affects water pollution. If she'd actually gotten her Ph.D., or shoot, even her master's, she would have probably been running her own damn program. Goals. Sometimes you can wrap up an entire ego inside a big whopping goal.

"You just said you haven't had a vacation in years. I never even had a real vacation."

"What? What, were you locked up or something? No, you're a doctor, right?" Elly pointed at the woman.

The woman laughed without mirth. Her voice was suddenly hoarse, as though her throat had been roughed up with sandpaper. "Locked up is a good way of putting it, but I don't want to discuss it anymore. I just thought since we were here together like this, sharing what little there might be to share, well." She sighed. "Forget it."

"No! Do not say 'forget it.' What are you getting at? Are you really thinking about not getting on the train?" Elly was wild with nervousness. Her stomach heaved and her pulse quickened. "Dammit. I think I have to throw up."

Elly got up and went past the dunes, out of sight of her companion. The dizziness, just like the dizziness that had spread over her this morning, came welling up, first in her stomach and then extending out to her limbs. She knelt down in the sand and retched a little, but nothing came up. All she had inside her belly was that cup of coffee she had two gulps of hours ago. Or was it days ago? A lifetime? She didn't want to think about these questions, so she straightened up and went back.

The woman with the dark hair had vanished. There were two slight indentations in the sand where her elbows had rested. Elly looked down the beach and could not see anyone in white. She sighed and felt more alone than ever before in her existence.

"Hi there."

Elly jumped at the voice. She turned around and saw a young man holding a fishing rod and a steel bucket. He smiled. "Sorry to scare you, miss, but you looked sort of lost."

He was wearing dark blue jeans faded white around the knees and rolled up around the ankles. A white T-shirt, like the kind her grandfather used to wear, was semi-tucked in around his waist. His skin was pockmarked and tan, his eyes brown and friendly. His black hair was streaked with fine gray hairs, but he looked to be only about twenty-eight or so.

"I didn't see you coming up the beach." She relaxed. "Did you catch anything?" she asked, leaning over and looking into the bucket.

"Just starting out. End of the day is the best time to find 'em. Name's Patrick. Pat," he said, nodding toward her.

Elly did not know whether she should say her name aloud or not. Would she jinx the dream if she became real to this man? "Elly. My name is Elly," she allowed. She smiled back at him and then looked away from his gaze.

"Haven't seen you around here before. You visiting from somewheres else?" he prodded, then just as quickly added, "No, you just ignore my busybody ways. That was sure impolite. Sorry."

"No. No. That's quite all right. Actually, I am visiting. From Seattle. I have some friends nearby, but I just wanted to wander around alone for a while. You know how it is." She wanted him to turn back to his walk to the shoreline and away from her.

He stayed put and just looked at her, smiling. Elly looked around for someone wearing white, but she was alone now; alone with Pat on a beach somewhere in the year 1942. The sun heated her head and it seemed the waves hit the beach louder than just moments ago. It was almost deafening. When he spoke next, she had to lean close to him to hear what he was saying.

"I wouldn't mind a little company while I set my line, if you're not too busy, that is."

Too busy? "Well, I do have a train to catch in a while," she said, thinking how polite and attractive this man was, "but sure. I've got some time to kill."

"Train? What train?" Pat asked her.

A black dot of panic hit Elly in her solar plexus and its warmth spread upward to her throat. "The one at the end of the road," she said, pointing toward the place she and the others met on the sand dunes.

The man laughed and started walking toward the ocean. "I don't know where you're going, but the trains stopped running these tracks about five years ago. But don't worry. If you need a lift somewhere, I can borrow my mother's car and get you to where you need to be after I catch some dinner. Come on now."

No reason to suspect it should be a real train if this is not reality, she speculated to herself. She took a few deep drags of the salty air and trotted after him. She watched quietly as he impaled a long squirming worm onto a hook and cast his line with a heavy weight on its end as far as it would reach into the breaking waves. Then he pushed the end of the rod into the moist sand, and sat down hard. He looked up at her and grinned. "Might be a while. Why not sit?"

Elly smiled and sat down next to Pat. The wind drifted his scent toward her and the musky smell of his sweat aroused her senses. "So, what do you do, Pat?"

"Do? Well, I fish a lot. When I'm not fishing I tend to my mother's needs mostly. She had a stroke some years back during the hurricane, and it's up to me, see, to make sure she's fed and cleaned up."

She wondered about the hurricane but thought it better not to mention it. "No one else in the family to help?"

"Got a sister, but she doesn't live anywhere near here. My two brothers are both off fighting the Krauts. Want a beer?" he asked, dipping his hand into the steel bucket and pulling out a long brown bottle.

"No, thanks. If you don't mind me asking, how come you're not off fighting too?"

"Bad ears. I had a really bad cold when I was a kid and it went into my drums. I can hear fine, if you ask me. Or go ahead and ask Mama. All she's got to do is whisper and I come running, even if I'm in the next room. But the Army tested me and said I'm below what's acceptable. Guess a man's got to be able to hear those orders real good or he's likely to go shooting the wrong people," he said, chuckling to himself.

Elly laughed along with him. "You're lucky."

Pat stopped grinning. "Lucky? It's lucky for Mama, sure, that I'm home with her. But it's no fun being the only guy from high school that's not out there in the world defending what's right." He took a long swig of his beer and wiped his lips with the back of his tanned hand. "Makes a man feel less like a man, if you know what I mean."

Elly smiled to herself. Not a lot of would-be heroes back home in her time looking for the right to defend anything other than their own individual rights. The right to make more money and the right to spend it on huge houses tucked safely behind steel gates. She gazed at the man to her right. He was so young and handsome. She imagined him in an Army uniform and wondered what it would have been like to be someone's sweetheart while he was overseas fighting. Would he put her photograph inside his helmet like she saw in the movies, and would she get chicken-scratched love letters smeared with the mud of the trenches?

"You are one of the prettiest girls I ever set eyes on, do you know that?"

Elly blushed. "What? Oh. Thank you." She had not

heard such a line in all her life, and it sounded perfect coming from this man perched behind a long wooden fishing pole.

"I apologize for being so forward. It's the beer that's talking is all. I wish more girls like you lived around here. How long you say you're visiting for?"

Elly wavered. "Only for a few more hours." She looked around the beach to see if any of her comrades were close by, but she spied only a few late-afternoon people left. Some napped in the fading sun. Most of the families were packing up their blankets and sun umbrellas. She suddenly felt so sad, as if someone she loved had died and she found out too late to say good-bye. "Do you know what time it is?"

"Five fifteen," Pat said. Elly did not quite get the flow of time today. It seemed to her she awoke in this dream reality maybe two, three hours ago, and she could have sworn it was early morning. Now she wished it was hours ago and that Pat had started fishing much earlier. She liked being next to him this way, just sitting and talking about the world. She had not been on a date in a while, and the last few had been so dismal and boring, they were not worth remembering. When was the last time I felt giddy just sitting with someone new and finding out about his life, she wondered. She wanted to sit here with Pat for hours more, maybe go home with him and eat the fish he catches with him and his mother. Make small talk about the war. She imagined after dinner they would clear the plates and sit around the radio in the warmth of a tiny living room, listening to the scratchy-sounding news. A crocheted blanket would warm her feet, and Pat would smoke a cigarette. His mother would be smiling at her.

So untouchable was this vision that she almost laughed aloud at her own foolish daydreaming. "How come you just stuck your head in a box?" Pat asked.

"What?"

"One minute you're sitting here next to me and the next thing you go and stop hearing me talk. Like you just disappeared right before my eyes. Am I boring you?"

Elly blushed. "No. You're right. I'm sorry. You are anything but boring. I was feeling a little sad that I have to leave so soon. I was really enjoying sitting here with you."

Pat leaned over before Elly had a moment to react, and put his right hand around her neck while lowering her slowly to the sand and kissing her lips, hard and closed-mouthed. She kissed him back with her eyes closed, thinking of *From Here to Eternity* and wondering if a wave would come in and lap at their bodies locked in passion.

Pat opened his eyes and stared down at her. He was smiling, and his eyes were shining with happiness; she could feel his excitement in his heart beating fast against her chest. He kissed her again.

This cannot be happening, Elly thought. Only I would find the perfect man in a dream. He felt so good against her that she ached to shove away her uncertainty and give in to his kisses.

At last he pushed himself away and pulled her up with him. His words came out in one quick breath. "I don't know what came over me, Elly. It's not like I'm some Casanova. I don't normally act like this around girls. I didn't mean to take advantage of you, really. Aren't you going to slap me?"

Elly laughed. "Slap you? Why would I do that?"

"For being such a heel. The last time I kissed a gal without her saying it was okay first, I got a real fast one across the cheek. It stung like heck, I can tell you."

Elly leaned closer to him and touched the cheek she suspected had stung like heck, and caressed it slowly and softly with the back of her hand. Then she kissed it. Before her face moved from his, Pat grabbed her close to him again and kissed her, with his mouth open and his tongue touching hers.

She hugged him, reaching around his back and clasping her hands together as if with them locked like that he would need a key to get out. He snuggled his face in her hair and breathed in so deeply that she was forced to let her hands part company. They looked at one another, as if for the first time.

"Who'd you say you were visiting?" Pat asked. He swept his dark hair off his face with his large hand, and she followed each knuckle bend and grace of his fingers. She liked the feel of that hand on her neck.

She conjured up a name from childhood. "Missy Laikes," she said, and looked at her feet, realizing she had no shoes on. What did he think, that she has nothing on her but the white dress she now wore?

"I was hoping it was someone I knew, someone from the neighborhood. I was going to go ask her to let me keep you for a while longer," Pat said with a childish smile.

Elly returned his crooked grin and let the moment go. She believed that if she shared too much, she would wake up and her Pat would be gone. She wanted to bask in the light of Pat's eyes for as long as time would allow. "Missy wouldn't take too well to that. I barely get to visit her as it is, what with being so far away." She realized she had no idea how far away she was talking about. She guessed from the accents she heard that she was on the East Coast—probably New England—but just to be sure, she looked out at the sea. She sighed. No setting sun to share with her new beloved, just fading light.

They sat silently for minutes, Pat stroking Elly's hand with his. He tugged at the fishing rod but without purpose. She turned his wrist and looked at the watch face, white with black numbers. A Timex. She wondered what Pat would think about the new Swatch watches. She had seen a cute one with fish on it just the other day in Nordstrom. He would laugh when he saw it and she would love buying it for him. She wanted to give him everything.

The hunger she felt surprised her, but she couldn't deflect it. Didn't want to. She reached her small hands up to each side of his face and pulled his mouth onto hers. She wanted him completely; wanted to lift her dress and pull him into her.

Pat opened his eyes and ended the kiss. "What color suit do you want me to wear to our wedding?" he asked, his right hand gently brushing Elly's hair away from her face.

"What?" she was so startled by the question, she grabbed his hand, stopped the motion mid-stroke. "Pat. I can't. You don't understand."

She looked at the Timex. 5:55.

She had to go.

"Pat. Listen. I have to leave now."

"What are you talking about? You're not going anywhere. You're staying here with me forever, and that's the way it is." He looked away from her, turned his head so far to the right, she could no longer see his eyes.

"This is crazy, Pat. We don't even know each other. I mean, we've literally known each other for what, forty minutes?"

"No," he said, pulling her against him, breathing his beer and salt breath into her face, "I've known you my whole life. I've waited for a girl like you to wash ashore and make someone like me happy. Elly, I've been so lonely. And here you are. My mermaid come to keep my heart warm. To ask me how my day went. To let me listen to her secrets." His face displayed so much hurt, Elly did not know what to do.

"You don't even know me, Pat. You don't know what you're saying," was all she could muster. Her heart was racing and her shoulders ached.

"I know how you smell," he said. "I know you're a dream come true."

She shook her head. This cannot be happening. How could I come to love someone so quickly? She toyed with the idea of staying. But that note the man found, You must be on it. The words splayed across her vision. What if she missed it? What was the worst that could happen? So what if this were real; couldn't she just stay here with Pat, start a new life? What about her family? What would happen to them? Would she just disappear or would it be that she never existed? Would those people in that white room come looking for her and tear her from her Pat and his mother? Would she die if she did not board that train?

She panicked. She had to be on that train, her gut called on her to act. Get on the train, her skin seemed to scream. Get on the train. She stood up and started to walk away. Pat got up after her and began following.

"You cannot come with me, Pat. I have to go. I'm sorry. Stay here!" she yelled at him. He followed her, leaving the fishing pole standing in the sand like a cross in the desert.

She ran and looked around for others in white. She saw no one but strangers. She reached the street and headed in the direction the note said to follow. Pat was close behind. She ran faster. She stopped when she saw the train ahead of her on rusty abandoned tracks. It was one car, a plain gray passenger-carrying module, just like any Amtrak train she had seen a hundred times in her life. But this one was not connected to another car. Alone it stood, in the middle of an old littered train yard, like a stray lamb standing idly under an oak, lost from its flock. The doors were open.

Pat ran into her and grabbed her by the upper arms. "You're crazy. Why did you run from me?" He finally noticed the train. "What? What's going on here? Why is that train car there? Is that the train you were talking about?" His face was a smear of confusion. His eyes worked against each other in concentration as he kept looking from Elly to the train.

"I have to go, Pat. I have to be on that train or, or something horrible could happen." Elly pulled away from his arms and saw the time on his watch. 6:10. "I'm sorry you followed me. This is as weird for me as it is for you, believe me," she said, holding his hand in hers and backing up in small steps.

"What's weird, Elly? That we just met each other, fell in love, and now you're leaving me? Or that train? That you're about to get on a train that has no engine attached to it and you think you're going to go somewhere?"

Elly felt the precious intensity between their bodies; she knew she could touch the air in front of his chest and sense the pulse of his heart. But it was too late to reach out her hand. She turned and ran up the stairs of the train.

They were all there. The men and women in white who landed with her on that beach this morning. They were talking as any other tourists might after a day of sightseeing apart from the group. She heard the man with the wild hair say, "I played with their kids and they fed me a tuna fish sandwich on Wonder Bread. I can't remember a tuna sandwich ever tasting so good."

The blonde woman was there, the one who wafted into the crowd of laughing soldiers on leave. In the momentary glimpse Elly had of her, she looked contented. They all looked so happy. She had just noticed that the dark-haired woman, her companion for part of the day, was missing, when Pat jumped on the train.

"What's he doing here? No strangers allowed!" one of the men yelled.

"Get him off the train!"

"Lady, what were you thinking letting him follow you here?" asked an elderly man she did not even remember from only hours ago. A frenzy of panicked talking and shouting started and Elly's breath came quickly from her mouth. "Pat, you have to get off this train. It could be dangerous, you being here." She pulled him with her and tried to drag him to the door.

He pressed her against the side of the train next to the steps, away from the other passengers, and leaned his face into hers. "I don't know what's going on here, but I think that beer did something mighty vicious to my brain." The door of the train began to close. "Those people there, it's like they're not real, like a hallucination. I thought you were one too when I saw you today, all dressed in white and the sun hitting you the way it did."

Elly was crying and the people behind her were still screaming for her to get the stranger off the train. The train started to heave forward and the passengers went silent in unison. They looked away from Elly and the man with her, out the window to the past they were leaving behind. A woman cried.

"I am real, Pat. But from another time. I live forty-eight years from now in the future. Pat, darling. Pat, are you listening to me?" He pushed himself against the door of the train, then frantically he was clawing to open it, but there was no give.

"My mother needs me!" he yelled. "I've gotta get off this train. Dear Jesus. God, please. Someone help me off this train!"

Elly pulled at the door with him, but the train had picked up speed. The scenery, normal green trees and picket fences surrounding cottages and shacks went by slowly. No one stood up to help. The others sat in their red leather seats, watching out the windows as if in a dream, now dazed and quiet, as if Pat and Elly were figments, not real. There was a sudden gust of sound, like a sonic boom, and as the train jerked forward Elly grabbed for a seat arm and saw Pat being thrown to the floor. The great moaning boom got louder and louder. She pushed her palms against her ears and just before she closed her eyes she saw Pat opening the door of the train.

Elly wakes up with her right cheek pressed against a smooth surface. She smells old wood and is vaguely aware that someone is talking loudly at her. In the background she hears Judy Garland singing a tune about someone leaving someone:

> There'll come a time, now don't forget it,
> There'll come a time, when you'll regret it
> Some day, when you grow lonely,
> Your heart will break like mine and you'll want me only,
> After you've gone,
> After you've gone away.

Elly opens her eyes and lifts her head slowly. Owen is looking down at her. Behind him, with their faces screwed up, a young couple is waiting at the counter with their arms crossed.

"Hey. Are you all right?" Elly realizes the boy is directing the question to her. She wipes her right hand across her face, breathes in, looks around the room.

"Yeah. Yeah, I'm fine. Sorry about that."

"Jesus. Your head dropped down so hard, I thought

maybe you got a concussion. Should I call an ambulance or something?"

"No. Thanks. I'm fine. Go back to what you were doing," Elly says. He turns his attention to the couple dressed in black.

"It was a dream," she whispers to herself. Yet it felt so unbelievably real. Tangible. She thinks her darling Pat was only a man of the moors, but when she bends her arm and smells the hollow space in front of her elbow, she swears she can smell his sweet sweat. Her heart burns and her throat is dry. She takes a sip of her hot coffee and breathes out, leaden with grief. Glancing at the couple at the counter, she sees at least a dozen pierced body parts between them. Elly wonders what Pat would have thought of pierced tongues and noses. She smiles a tiny smile as a teardrop falls from her face and lands on the blue notebook filled with statistics on urban car-washing habits.

Elly is lying on her futon bed, staring out the window toward downtown Seattle, when the phone rings. It is her former Environmental Policy professor and friend, Rochelle Hitchcock. Even though Elly bowed out of her second try at a graduate program rather ungracefully (halfway through the last quarter), Rochelle does not make Elly feel guilty about failing. No, that is her father's goal in life.

She wants to tell Rochelle about the dream, Pat, the

train, the horrible afterthoughts that are slicing her insides apart. How she senses a phantom love, like an invisible indentation made on the pillow next to her. Before she even begins the story Rochelle informs Elly that she has about thirty-nine seconds to talk, invites her to a dinner party she and her fiancé, Phillip, are throwing in celebration of someone's promotion at the university, and hangs up.

Elly is seated next to Phillip's friend Joseph Connelly, a history professor at San Francisco State University. He is here in Washington interviewing for a teaching position at Seattle Pacific University. Elly likes him immediately. He is older than she, in his forties, but he is unusually fit and strong. He laughs at everything, a hearty, deep laugh that makes her giggle along with him, even when the moment is not the least bit humorous. He has jet-black hair and rugged acne-scarred skin. The way he looks away when he is thinking softens her heart to him instantly. When she speaks, his attention turns rapt; she feels his brown eyes linger on her face just a few seconds too long.

After the overdone flan, Rochelle suggests everyone meet at the new Cajun Corner club for beer and dancing. The Seattle night is cold and damp, but the air inside the bar is warm. Tropical red and yellow neon lights blaze around the room as Cajun music blasts from the speakers. Joseph asks Elly to dance. He takes her right hand and they step onto the floor.

Still holding one hand together, they sway playfully as an accordion squeaks out zydeco rhythms.

"It's a dream of mine to visit New Orleans," Elly tells Joseph.

"Go with me next week," Joseph says to her, tossing his hips in time to the song. Elly smiles at the way he so casually assumes she will go with him, and chuckles at him with a flip of her hair to the beat of the music. He stops dancing and looks at her.

"I'm serious. Let me take you to New Orleans," he says.

She knows he is serious, but she does not want to go. She feels suddenly vulnerable and she pushes away from the dance floor, where she leaves him dancing with Phillip and two other women from the dinner party. She sits down at the small wrought iron table with Rochelle, and takes a long drink of her Pike Place Ale.

"He's nice, isn't he?" Rochelle asks Elly.

"Yeah. I like him, but there's something about him. . . ."

"What? That's a little scary? A little intense?" says Rochelle. "I know it. It's the God thing. He had a very weird childhood, from the few things Phillip's told me about him. He is extremely religious and I think it makes him feel invincible, you know? Plus, he's going through this pretty sad divorce. He didn't tell you?"

Elly shakes her head.

"Don't tell him I told you."

Elly ignores the divorce comment. "Religious?" He has not said a word all night that would lead her to believe that. No cross around his neck. No abstention, that's for certain. Huh. She looks at him, dancing with some other woman from the group, and squints her eyes hoping to get him more into focus.

They leave in separate cars, but not before he takes her hand in his one last time. "We won't always have New Orleans, but maybe someday we'll have somewhere else."

He leaves a rose with a note, "Remember me with this red rose," in front of her door on the day he returns home to California. In the days and weeks that follow, he phones her and they talk about their days, their menial routines. He writes her letters; stories, really. Stories of his childhood. And his passions; first religious, and finally ones directed toward her.

January 23, 1991

Dear Elly,

It was a Dickens of a Christmas in San Francisco.

That is to say, it was the best of Christmases, it was the worst of Christmases.

This year, the first song the church choir sang was an old English carol, "Winter Passes Over," by Purcell. It's a simple, pretty air, the kind you might expect a group of neighborhood carolers to sing (if your neighborhood happens to be somewhere in the vicinity of Cornwall, that is). It was a safe song to start the concert with because it had a real easy part—there wasn't much chance that I would make any glaring errors. All I had to do was keep my voice soft and let the bass section leader carry our part.

The best part of the song for me came right at the very end. The song tells the story of the three kings (also known as the three wise men), who travel from distant lands to visit the Christ child. When the kings finally arrive where the infant is lodging, the song reaches a roaring crescendo, with a chorus of angels imploring the kings to, "Come in! Come in, ye kings!"

Then, suddenly, dramatically, the song pauses. The sanctuary grows very quiet. The anticipation is tremendous. The audience waits anxiously for the choir to continue. And gently, softly, the sopranos and altos pick up the tune. "And kiss the feet of God," they whisper.

As they hold their last note, the men quietly, reverently echo their final two words: "Of God." It sounds very straightforward. The only tricky part is that the bass note is a low B-flat, which is the musical equivalent of Death Valley. A low B-flat is so low, no one can actually hear it. One kind of feels it instead.

I don't know why, but almost every time I've broken up with someone in the past thirty years, it's been during the Christmas season. With the exception of two or three breakups that have occurred right around Easter. (As you have suspected, I'm a religious kind of guy.)

I kept my record intact this year. Just before Christmas, Catherine came out for a visit. Separation was supposed to make our hearts grow fonder, but hey, not all myths are true. Never let it be said that divorce is an easy way out.

We did our bit for Dickens.

January 29, 1991

Dear Elly,

So I'm back in the Midwest for a week, back in the land where I grew up.

It made me homesick for California. In fact, when I got to the hotel, I drove back and forth over the speed bumps a few times. It was the closest I could get to the Santa Cruz Mountains.

My moral development peaked in twelfth-grade sociology class.

At the beginning of the school year, our instructor, Mr. Clarke, announced that much of our class grade would be based on a number of projects that we would conduct in teams of two.

Usually I was medium-popular in school, but on this occasion I was hot shit. I had a reputation as a brainiac, and everybody in the class decided I was a sure ticket to an A. Jocks wanted to be my partner.

Cheerleaders wanted to be my partner. I got more partnership offers than United Airlines.

Instead, though, I did something crazy. In the midst of the wheeling-and-dealing frenzy, I turned to Becky Bennett, who was seated behind me, and I asked, "Would you be my partner, Becky?"

To grasp the significance of this, you have to picture Becky. Can you imagine Roseanne Barr with pimples and no personality? Well, that was Becky— and I believe I'm being charitable here.

After seeing Becky alone so often, both at school and walking home, I was sure she had no close friends. Perhaps she kept to herself because she was confident of her ability to face life alone, because she found her meditations and daydreams more stimulating than conversations with hormone-crazed delinquents.

Maybe it was my curiosity that prompted me to ask Becky to be my partner in class that day. Perhaps there was a bit of altruism involved too; maybe I wanted Becky to have a friend, in case she ever needed one. Perhaps I hoped both of us would benefit from our relationship.

What I didn't expect was that Becky would hesitate to accept my offer. I expected her to shout and leap with joy. Here I was saving her from the humiliating task of finding someone who would be her partner, plus I was practically guaranteeing that she would receive an A. How could she help but be enthusiastic?

But there was no joy in Becky-ville that day. Instead, she said nothing, she betrayed no emotion. Her catatonic stare lasted 5, 10, 15 seconds. Then softly, almost inaudibly, Becky told me, "Yes." Not, "Yes, thank you." Nor, "Yes, I appreciate it." But, "Yes." Simply, "Yes."

I wondered if she felt any emotion.

Each day I said hi to her, but only rarely did she respond in kind. Even when we prepared together to lead a class discussion, Becky rationed her speech. She never qualified a comment when a simple "yes" or "no" would do. Her Mount Rushmore expression made it impossible to read her mind.

The school year flew past. We seniors made decisions that would determine our fates. College and work plans were crystallized. Finals were a week away, and then there was graduation.

During the last sociology class period, Mr. Clarke gave us an inspirational speech. (He was the football coach too, so I suppose it was something he felt obligated to do.) We jiggled anxiously in our seats until the final bell rang, when we whooped and hollered for joy. "All riiiiight!" Tom Mounce shouted as we slapped hands.

The shouting slowly died. As I reached under my desk to collect my notebooks and gear for the final time, I felt a gentle tapping on my arm. It could have been a fly or a mosquito, and I was tempted to brush it away. But out of the corner of my eye, I saw Becky's outstretched hand. While the rest of the class was milling and celebrating, Becky alone remained seated.

"I wanted to tell you," she whispered, "that you're different from all these people. Every day you said hello and were nice to me. You're my friend, Joe. Thanks for being my friend."

I thanked her back. I patted her on the arm. It was surprisingly soft. "You're my friend too," I assured her.

Mark dropped us off in order, per usual. Pete left first, then Tom, and finally me.

I bounded in the back door, yelled "Hi!" to my aunt, and charged downstairs to my bedroom in the basement. I threw my books on the nightstand, sat down on my bed, and pulled my pillow out from under the covers. I squeezed the pillow closely to my chest. I took a deep breath and sighed.

Then I cried for fifteen minutes because Becky was my friend.

Joseph

He ran into his aunt's house. Why was he living at his aunt's? Why on earth am I curious about this? she wonders. So what if he doesn't talk of his family. It's not like I've said a word about my own. Yet his past gnaws at her more than her reasoning understands.

March 8, 1991

Dear Elly,

I decided to visit the beach today.

I know I said last week that I prefer the Atlantic to the Pacific. That's because I'm basically a lazy good-for-nothing slob. The Atlantic has all sorts of beaches where you can plunk yourself down on a blanket, open a trashy book, and fall asleep while you bake. The Pacific has far fewer beaches of that sort, at least here in northern California, where the temperature near the ocean rarely rises above 60°.

On the other hand, today there is nowhere I would rather be than the Pacific. It is a misty gray, rainy day. The tide is beating powerfully against the shore. I am tucked inside a tiny little cave that the surf has carved out of the cliffs along the beach. It's a cozy spot, sheltered from the elements, the perfect size for a picnic and a mid-afternoon snuggle.

I was born on the Atlantic, did you know that?

Have I told you yet that I feel very connected to you? Even when you surprise and titillate me (I love that word) when we're talking on the phone, it feels kind of cozy and warm, like a wild and crazy friend whom I've known forever. I hate to lapse into clichés like "chemistry" and "electricity," but how else can I describe the thrill?

Maybe in time we'll become even better friends. Maybe your yin will figure out my yang.

Maybe we'll build a legacy along the way. Or maybe we'll just create our own little legacies.

I am wondering what will happen when we see each other again.

Joseph

He calls her in March. "Hi, I'll be up in a couple of weeks for Phil and Rochelle's wedding. Want to be my date?"

"Of course I do," she says into the green plastic phone. She should be happier, more excited. But like a hundred times before, the image of Pat stains her emotions. Since awakening from the dream, she remembers daily the feeling of his lips on hers, the pressure of his body, his shy laugh. He was just a dumb New England hick, she reminds her imagination. Okay, so what if he had been real? I'd marry him and end up washing his mother's underwear for the next twenty years. His brothers would come home from the war and we'd all sit around every night telling stories. I would make meat loaf and Pat would rub my neck while I stood at the sink doing dishes. Then, after his brothers went home and his mother dozed in front of the radio, he'd take me tight in his arms, kiss my eyes first, then my cheek, softly. Then he'd move his lips to my neck, his hands playing under my shirt—

"You there?" he asks.

"Yes, silly. I'm here. Just saw something strange out my window."

"What color suit should I wear? God forbid I clash with you," he teases into the phone.

Sweet, caring Joseph. How could she not feel love for him? She is putting on a vivacious front for him, and he is buying it, obviously grateful for being cared about. And from her end, well, she wants someone to need her love. Other than Rochelle, she has no one willing to hear past the sound of her voice when she talks. The people at work shuffle their papers in time to one another. Her father calls less than once a month now that he is no longer checking up on her academic progress. "Your mother and I wonder why you bothered with this whole education thing in the first place. You knew you were never going to make it as a, what the hell was that, environmental manager," he bellows across the miles of copper phone wire.

Joseph buzzes her apartment on Friday morning. As she waits for the elevator to climb five floors and screech to a stop, she prays for infinite love. She opens the door and immediately knows that there will be no duration, but his smile is so bright that she is helpless to do anything but hug him back.

Heading out to Whidbey Island, they lean their elbows on the cold railings of the ferry and watch the land shrink before them. A bald eagle flies by at eye level and Elly's breath is stuck in her throat. She wants Joseph to kiss her. On the water like this, the frigid wind tearing at their backs, Elly leans into Joseph's warmth and forgets, for the moment, her doubts. She allows Pat to blur.

They check into their room at the Inn at Penn Cove. The air is laden with potpourri and there are three antique porcelain dolls seated perfectly on a child's wooden chair.

"I missed you," Joseph says, tying his shoelaces and getting ready to go join the others for the pre-wedding picnic. "But I think there's too much space between us. Did this grow too quickly?"

Elly sighs. "You have the most beautiful way of saying the shittiest things. I don't know. I mean, I really care for you, and in here"—she points to her stomach—"you're the one. Like I've known all my life I'd meet you. But in here"—the finger moves five inches higher—"well, it's not as full as it should be." She sits hard on the four-poster mahogany bed. "Does that make any sense?"

"Clearer than the view out this window. Listen, darling." He sits next to her, his smell makes Elly's eyes half close. "I have no great investment here. You're wonderful and then some, but it's not like I've been shopping for a ring. I've got this new job starting in the summer—"

"You got the job?"

"Yes. I've known for a while. I didn't tell you because I didn't want you to feel any pressure."

"Wow. Then you'll be living here."

Joseph turns Elly's face to his. "Just because I'm going to be living here does not mean we have to become lovers. Not that I wouldn't love that. I pray for it all the time. But Elly, I'm still reeling from the divorce. How about we just let the fates decide?"

"That sounds good to me," Elly says, and together they run to the shoreline, where the barbecue is smoking and friends of Phillip and Rochelle are celebrating.

Throughout the day Elly watches Joseph talk to people. He makes everyone laugh. He stares at her whenever he has a free moment to look away from his conversation, and she feels as if she is being followed. Phillip puts his arm across Joseph's shoulders and the two of them go off for a walk together. She wants to accompany them, hear their intimacies, the sort shared only by two childhood friends.

They get into the same bed that night. They kiss. Again and again. He removes her shirt and her underwear. He moves his head down over her stomach, breathing unevenly and expectantly. She stops him. "I cannot do this," she says, and feels once again like she is in high school in the backseat of a borrowed car.

"It was worth a try," Joseph utters, his pride not the slightest tinged. "You have mighty fine skin. At least you left me with a good taste in my mouth. Here." He puts his arm around her back and pulls her head into the crook between his shoulder and chest. "Let's just be here together for a while, shall we?"

Elly is content and the embarrassment of feeling like a tease soon fades. She rubs her palm along his chest and thinks of his kindness. "Were your parents nice people?" she finally asks.

"I don't know," he returns coldly, "I never knew my parents."

"You're adopted?" She feels his body tense and the soft hold of his arms falls away completely.

"Adopted. Abandoned. All the same, right?"

Elly sits up quickly and looks at him. "I'm sorry, Joseph. I didn't mean to bring this up. Let's just forget about it."

But it is too late. He is already thinking about it. He leans to the floor to grab a sweatshirt. He stands and puts on his blue jeans too.

"Where are you going?" Elly asks. She stands and begins dressing as well.

"For a walk. Want to come?"

The night is clear and quiet; all the island's inhabitants and guests are inside. Most of the few homes and inns in the small community are dark, but some windows reflect the glare of television sets. Still, Elly feels oddly like she did in her dream. As if she is walking among strangers, real yet verging on invisible. A mirage on the landscape. The memory of the dream courses through her and she is uncomfortable walking alongside Joseph at the water's edge.

The tide is out and the moon's light washes over the shoreline. The sounds of the water lapping in and out are lonely sounds, as if the waves come looking for an answer and finding only blackness, recede away disappointed.

"I never knew my mother," Joseph begins. "And what I know about my father isn't the kindest of stories. What I do know, my aunt Lois told me, but after she told me the whole story, she also forbade me from asking any questions. Being the good kid that I was, I let it go. For a time, anyway."

They walk across the sand to the rocks lining the beach and sit watching the silent horizon. Joseph thinks something to himself and laughs.

"What?" Elly perks up. "Why do you even want to talk to me about this?"

Joseph laughs again, but there is little cheer in his throat. "I don't know. I always seem to think about my parents whenever I get involved with someone new. Why you? Because I trust you. Because I tasted your skin. Because I know from your not-so-subtle questions on the phone that you're interested. Shit." He wipes his large flat hands across his eyes. Elly cannot see if his skin comes away wet. "Because I feel like it. Is that okay with you?"

Elly nods silently. She lets the words come as he wishes they should.

"My parents met in Mystic, Connecticut. No one has told me much about my mom, her name was Iris, like the flower. Or the eye part. I'm not sure. Anyway, the way they met is really weird. Everything I know about them is weird, so if I stop making sense, just let me finish before you ask me any questions, okay?"

"Yes. Sure," Elly answers, curious now and more afraid of the darkness out there than moments before.

"The way Aunt Lois tells it is that one summer day Dad goes off fishing like he always did late in the afternoons. He takes care of their mom, his and Lois's, since Lois lives in Iowa with her husband and their two brothers are off in the armed forces."

Elly is anxious.

"Only he doesn't come back like he always does around six or seven or so, to make dinner. He just disappeared. Well, his mom, my grandmother, gets all nervous and phones some neighbors to go down to the beach and look for him. She can't walk herself because she had a stroke. So, after a while some people come knocking at her door and tell her there's no sign of her son."

Elly is terrified. Her heart is slamming into her chest. She is having trouble breathing.

"One of the neighbors says he thinks he saw my dad walking down toward the old train station, but wasn't sure it was him. So everyone just waits a little while before calling the police. Well, another day goes by and my grandmother is thinking that maybe he got himself drunk or something, but it wasn't like him to be so irresponsible. Everyone knew he was really good about taking care of his mother. She calls my aunt in Iowa and Aunt Lois tells her to call the cops. So she does. But they find nothing."

"Is he gone for good?" Elly is in a panic. The blood in her temples is close to bursting past the skin's surface. She wonders, as if she could possibly wonder if the earth is flat, if she killed her friend's father. She is afraid to hear the name spoken aloud.

"No, not for good. But a long time. Aunt Lois comes and takes care of their mom for a while, until one of their brothers, my uncle Mike, gets discharged from the Army after getting shot in the hip. Lucky thing the guy didn't die. Remind me to tell you about Uncle Mike sometime. He's a funny guy."

"Okay," Elly says, but she is not thinking about Uncle Mike. She is awaiting the fate of Pat, Joseph's father. Her Pat, from the dream. It can't be, she assures herself briefly, but cannot outrun the certainty raging up on her. It is useless, she thinks, like trying to outski a speeding avalanche of wet and heavy snow that is soon to suffocate her.

"Mike comes back home and Aunt Lois goes back to Iowa and her family. Dad is just presumed drowned for the time being. See, they found his fishing pole still stuck into the sand. That and his bucket of beer. Everyone thought maybe he got drunk and went for a swim but didn't come out of the water.

"Grandmother got so sick over missing him, she died sooner than she should have, given her health. Her doctor said she should have lived a long time, but her heart was broken over Dad being gone. Until her dying day, my aunt Lois told me, Grandmother never believed her son was dead."

No, he was taking a train into limbo instead, thought Elly. He followed me onto the train and I shouldn't have let him. It's my fault. All of this, it's my fault. Tears start welling up in her eyes, but she keeps her tiny whimpers quiet and lets Joseph continue.

"Five years go by and it's just Uncle Mike living in the house now."

"What about the other brother?"

"Killed in Normandy. Uncle Fred."

"Sorry."

"Hey, it wasn't like I ever knew him. But thanks. Aunt Lois didn't much like to talk about Fred. He was the baby brother and it was bad enough losing one. Two made her go a little crazy, I guess. She had his picture on the wall by our kitchen and every morning when she passed it, she would kiss her fingertip and touch the surface of the photo. Not my dad's, though. There were no pictures of him."

"You have no photographs of your dad?" Elly is dying to see her love Pat again, even in two dimensions.

"Sure, I've got a couple, but Aunt Lois, what with the scandal. Well, she never stopped being mad at him."

"How come?" Elly is close to breaking.

"Didn't we agree no questions till I finish? Sorry. I didn't mean to snap at you. This is just a little less than fun for me. That's all. Don't take it personally."

Personally? How could she take it otherwise? Her fingertips feel sorrow and her elbows know confusion. Elly is drowning.

"So, Uncle Mike is hanging out in the front yard one day, sitting on a lounge chair drinking a beer and reading the paper, when out of nowhere this woman shows up with a baby."

"What?"

"Elly, please." He takes in a gulp of salty air and swallows hard. She can see the pain in his face. "She has this baby, and she just hands it over to Uncle Mike. Just like that, and she starts walking away, but Uncle Mike jumps up and goes after the woman. He stops her before she's even made a few steps and drags her back to the yard. She's just staring at the baby and Uncle Mike is asking her all kinds of questions, but she's not listening. He starts yelling, 'Who are you? Whose baby is this? Lady, can you hear me?' Finally she looks up from the baby and says, 'This is your brother's baby. I wanted to keep him, but that would be dishonest. So here I am. I'm giving him to you.'

"Uncle Mike just about has a heart attack. He pushes the woman inside the house with him. He sits her down and puts the baby back in her arms. He paces up and down the room for a while, scratching his head, not knowing what to do."

Elly is becoming unhinged. Her throat is constricting and she fears she will black out before the story is complete. Joseph throws the rock he had been rubbing between his hands for the last few minutes into the surf. They both hear the tiny *plunk*.

"She tells Uncle Mike that about five years ago while she was working as a nurse in a hospital over in Mystic, about ten miles from the house, the police drag this man in one day and he's all scruffy and crazy-looking, screaming about a train. She said that he kept insisting that he just jumped off this train that took him away from his mother and now he's in the future. He kept repeating over and over that the year was 1990, or, hey—that's just last year."

Last year. Or forty-nine years ago. Elly is pinching her ankle through her socks. She is trying to wake up from this nightmare.

"She and some other nurses tried to soothe him, tell him he's not in the future, but he wouldn't hear them. They checked for some sort of ID on him, but his pockets were empty. So, they did what most hospitals would have done in the forties, they had him restrained. They put him in the psych ward and left him there. It was so busy that week, and she assumed someone else would try and find his family for him, but the days just went by and no one paid him much attention. One of the doctors looked in on him and asked his name, but he just screamed, 'Ask her. Ask the girl on the beach!' "

The girl on the beach is thinking about killing herself. What has she done? Oh, God. Is this hell?

"The nurse asked the cops if they could help find his family, but it was a different state from the one that had the report that my dad was missing. No computers back then. You would think they'd call around to see if this guy matched the description of someone who's missing, but no, they didn't bother checking. Too stupid or too lazy. Who knows.

"Dad languishes in this ward for a couple of years. No one makes any attempt to find out where he belongs. Can you believe that? No one. But this nurse who first saw him is sitting at the bar one night after her shift and she's telling some friends of hers about the guy who thinks he's living in the future, because she still finds the whole thing disturbing and she likes talking about him. This woman who is sitting alone at the next table looks over and asks a couple of questions about the guy. The nurse tells her his story and then this lady says thanks and leaves.

"The next day that same woman shows up at the hospital and asks if she can volunteer with the patients. She says she has experience working with crazy people and they let her hang out and play games with the folks on the psych ward. This nurse tells Uncle Mike that this woman, Iris, spends most of her time with my dad, talking softly to him, whispering soothing words that calm him. Everyone is glad she's there because the man is starting to be less crazy with her around. One day they're caught kissing in his room."

"Kissing?" Elly is hysterical. She is jealous that Pat would fall for another woman, but what is she thinking? She no longer existed for him. Did she ever exist in his life, or is this a horrible coincidence? "Sorry." She drops her head like a bad dog. "Go on."

"Not only kissing, it turns out. Iris got pregnant and when she began to show, the doctors ordered her out of the hospital. They threatened to press charges. Rape of men wasn't really an issue back then, so I think it would have been something like patient endangerment.

"Months later she crawls into the same hospital. She's in labor. The nurse is there, the same one as before. She's in the delivery room with Iris, who was bleeding pretty badly. Hemorrhaging, actually. The doctors were about to put her under with anesthesia, but right before they did, she grabbed the nurse's dress and pulled her close to her mouth. 'The baby's father is the man you have locked up here. His name is Pat McClary. Find his family. They live over in Watch Hill. In Rhode Island.' And then she was under.''

Pat. He spoke his name. Elly already knows what happened next.

"She died. But the baby lived. Lucky him. Lucky me. The nurse took me to Uncle Mike's and told him the whole story. She said she showed me to Pat, but he was still babbling about the train. He said he had to find his wife.

"Uncle Mike was frantic. He finds out his brother is alive and has a son. He tried to get the woman to wait while he called Aunt Lois in Iowa, but she got up to leave. He asked her if she had a photograph of my mother, Iris, and she pulled out her hospital ID card and told him it was all she could find on her. She had gone to the apartment address on her application form and found nothing else personal. 'Nothing,' she said.''

Elly hesitates. "What did she look like? Your mom?"

Joseph laughs. "A lot like me. I mean, really dark hair. What's strange is that there is no record of her. I searched all the libraries for anything to do with an Iris living in Connecticut, but I couldn't even find a birth record. I think she used a fake name.

"Uncle Mike calls Lois, who tells him to wait for her

so they could go and get Pat together. She makes it to Rhode Island a few days later and they go to the hospital to get their brother, only the lady at the desk tells them he'd checked himself out of the hospital just yesterday. They thought he was being held there, but the clerk told them he was free to go anytime. Do they know where he went? No. Some responsible folks, huh? They look everywhere, showing his picture to everyone on the street and they filed yet another missing persons complaint with the police.

"They all agreed that the best thing would be for Aunt Lois and her husband, my uncle Ken, to adopt me. I grow up in Iowa and know nothing about nothing until I'm sixteen, when my parents sit me down and tell me the truth."

Elly has to vomit but needs to hear the rest of the story first. She swallows the stinging bile that forms in her throat.

"It was shocking, to say the least. It was probably best they waited until then. My aunt was so upset, she told me it was okay if I wanted to start calling her Aunt Lois instead of Mom. I couldn't do it to her face, but inside, I no longer thought of these people as Mom and Dad."

The name Pat McClary is stuck in her gullet like a sideways fishbone. "Your dad then . . ." Elly hesitates. "Did you ever find him?" Her breath is short and weak and she wants to get up and run back to the room alone, get into the bed and cover her body with the down comforter. She needs only to fall asleep so that she might wake up again and know this was just a part of that same dream she had ages ago. It has to be, she tells herself, but the veracity of her thought lies limp in her brain.

"I did. I flew to Rhode Island when I was in my twenties. It didn't take that much work, you know? I figured he'd be living somewhere close to Watch Hill, since that was familiar to him. I also knew from Aunt Lois that he loved the ocean, so I skimmed all the little beach towns and found him living in a cabin in Weekapaug Beach, some five miles away. He's an alcoholic, totally disoriented, but I also think he's schizophrenic, although he wouldn't let me bring him in for any analysis. I tried, Elly. Oh God, I tried with all I had inside me. He didn't know me, want to know me. It was horrible."

He is crying now. Wracked with her own dangerously paranoid feelings, she still reaches out to him, hugs him close. He is drained. Her body is shocked. Together like this they get up and walk back to the inn together. They reach their room and as Joseph begins to undress, Elly asks him if he has the photo of his mother in his wallet. He says he does and reaches into the back of his pants. She knows before he hands it to her who she is.

Elly holds her right hand on the side of the cold porcelain sink and spits toothpaste foam at the drain. In the distance she hears some news person talking about President Bush's environmental record. Instinctively she knows this should be interesting, but it is enough to swallow without gagging.

At work Elly crunches data on sewage effluent and summarizes it into a report coherent enough for a monkey to understand. Her boss tells her he is happy with her work and gives her a raise. She thanks him and goes home. She turns on the television, takes off her red wool sweater, rolls it into a ball, and lies down, tucking it under her neck.

She tells no one of her bizarre experience. She fights with herself. Does she owe it to Joseph to tell him the truth; that she is the reason for his father's misery? She consoles herself every day that Joseph is alive only because of the dream, because the dark-haired woman made it to the beach that day along with the others. Since the wedding, he calls her less than he used to. Every time he does, his voice whittles away at her sanity and strength.

"Elly. What's up?"

"Nothing, Joseph. Just really busy at work."

"The moving van arrives on Tuesday next week. Want to help me unpack?"

"As much as I'd like to, you know how it is," Elly says, barely able to keep her shoulders from falling forward onto the floor.

Finally she lets Joseph evaporate from her life like water in a puddle after a day of sunshine. He does not fight to stay.

. . .

Time edges past her and Elly awakens from sleep and moves her right hand across her eyes. Pulling on the gray sweatpants that are lying on the floor, she attempts to unknot the white string, but gives up and lets the pants sag around her jutting hips. She slips the tiny gold key into the number 5 mailbox on the bottom floor, bunches the envelopes into the pocket of her fleece jacket, and walks the three blocks to the Krazy Kat Kafe, where she orders a double cappuccino. She takes her coffee to the table in the back and pulls out the mail. There is a wedding invitation. Joseph is getting married. She calls to congratulate him.

"Hi, Joseph. I got the invitation. It's very pretty. I'm sort of surprised you're inviting me, after, you know."

She hears him smile on the other end. "You're one of the reasons I was happy to move to Seattle in the first place. Maybe I shouldn't be telling you that, what with that big ego of yours."

"Yeah, huge. You can never add too much to it, you know."

"I know. I was just kidding. Look, it all turned out for the best anyway. I really want to thank you for bringing me up here so I could meet Kim."

"She's great, huh?"

"The best there is. And she knows all about you, so

don't worry about acting nonchalant when you see us. Are you coming?"

"Depends on where you registered for your gifts." She attempts humor, although a headache is starting to form on the left side of her brain. "Of course I'll come."

"Great. Oh, you'll get to meet my dad."

The sound of blackness rushes between Elly's ears. She sits down hard.

"Yeah, he finally got himself together and wants to come for the wedding."

"Really," she whispers.

"Okay, I'm exaggerating. He's not really together in the full sense of the word. But I took Kim out to Rhode Island with me a couple of months ago. She convinced me I had to try again to make him a part of my life. And she was so right.

"He's still living in that shack by the beach, and he's in and out of total clarity, but he's working part-time at a hardware store and gave up drinking entirely. He hasn't talked to anyone in the family, but he says he's ready to meet everyone. You can imagine how thrilled my aunt and uncles are."

Elly is careful. She watches her own reflection in the hallway mirror as she asks, "Does he still talk about the train incident?"

"Sort of. That's funny you bring it up. He refuses to

let me fly him out, so he's going to take Amtrak. When I wrote him about making reservations, he never wrote back. I finally spoke with him on the phone where he works. He said he was frightened of taking the train."

"Uh-huh. What'd you say?"

"I figured it was his mental illness acting up again, but I told him not to worry. He said it would be the second train ride he's ever taken in his life and he hopes this one won't kill him the way the first one did. I'm hoping to get him to stay here and then we can get him some real psychiatric help."

"That would be a good thing," Elly says.

Time slows to a drag and reality feels like a heavy backpack on her shoulders. She will see Pat again. Her love, Pat.

When the day of the wedding arrives, Elly wakes from her sleep. She is awake, yet still asleep. As if in a dream she dresses herself in a beige and pink calf-length cotton dress. She pulls her hair into a bun, then unwraps it and lets it fall to her shoulders. She changes her shoes twice and wipes the sweat from her underarms.

Pat.

She closes the door to her studio apartment on East Howell Street, where sunshine cuts past the Space Needle, pierces her window, and lands across the computer keyboard. She begins the eight-block walk to the church. There are voices in her head that she only slightly recognizes. They are probing her, throwing questions at her like darts against a cork wall. What will he say when he sees me? Will I make him more confused than he already is? Am I being totally selfish by going to this wedding? No, she thinks, I cannot do this to him. She stops at the bottom of Pine Street and turns back toward home.

As she crosses the Pine Street overpass, she pauses to watch the traffic on I-5 below her. The speeding cars are almost deafening, yet the continuous rush, the whoosh, mimics the beating of an exposed heart in an open chest. Whoosh. Whoosh. Whoosh. Whoo—

"Excuse me." Someone has approached and her chest closes back up again.

"Yes," she replies without turning her head to see the person in his entirety.

The voice is polite, but overly excited. "Is it true there's a place around here where you can see live salmon, you know, the fish, while they swim upstream to spawn?"

Elly detects something odd in his question and turns her attention to him now. "Sure," she utters. "Over at the Ballard Locks. You can take the bus, but . . ."

It dawns on her that he is wearing white pants. And a white T-shirt. She hesitates before looking down.

He is barefoot.

"Are you . . . ?" She cannot continue. She does not want to know.

"Thank you, but I can find it on my own. Must run. Not a lot of time, you know," he says and walks quickly into the heart of the city, camouflaged among the many world travelers and barefoot backpackers.

The rest of the day passes in slow motion. She watches the people walk by on the street beneath her window, and each one is Pat. As he was in 1942. She sleeps in fits and dreams of drowning, salt water stinging her eyes and lungs and the roof of her mouth as she gasps toward the surface of the ocean.

Elly's eyes open and there is the sound of car engines and a radio, yes, there is a radio playing music somewhere in the background. She thinks for a panicked second she is back in the dream, but sees that she left her stereo on the night before, trying to let the music calm her fraying edifice. The telephone is ringing.

"Hello?"

It is Rochelle. "Elly? What happened? How come you didn't come yesterday?"

Elly is tired. "I got sick. I felt like I got hit with the flu. I think I have a fever." She hesitates and hears Rochelle's curious breath. "How was it?"

"Beautiful and sad. I guess you didn't hear."

"Hear what?"

"Joseph went to pick his dad up from the train station

Saturday night, and when he and Kim got there, there was a whole bunch of police and fire engines around."

Elly knows. She is beyond feeling sad. She is lost beyond finding.

"He died on the train. I guess he had a heart attack just as they were pulling into the station. It was pretty devastating to Joseph."

"But they had the wedding anyway," says Elly.

"Yeah. They figured he would have wanted that. The priest said a really beautiful prayer for him. Everyone was crying. Kind of a crummy way to start off a marriage, if you ask me. But they had to think about their own happiness, of course."

"Of course," Elly repeats. Heat radiates from the plastic phone. It is burning her hand. She looks out the window toward the Space Needle and notices that it is falling over. The phone is melting into hot liquid goo in her right hand and her head is humming. She knows she is going to fall, so she aims her body toward the floor, away from the sharp corner of the TV stand. She is glad she does not hit her head. It is her last thought.

Elly awakens with her right cheek pressed against a smooth surface. She smells old wood and is vaguely aware that someone is talking loudly at her. Louis Armstrong is singing something about being harassed by the police for standing on a corner. Elly opens her eyes and lifts her head. Owen is looking down at her.

Behind him, a young man and woman, both dressed in black, are waiting at the counter with their arms crossed.

"Hey. Are you all right?" Elly realizes the boy is directing the question to her. She wipes her right hand across her face, breathes in, looks around the room.

"Yeah. Yeah, I'm fine. Sorry about that."

"Jesus. Your head dropped down so hard, I thought maybe you got a concussion. Should I call an ambulance or something?"

"No. Thanks. I'm fine. Go back to what you were doing," Elly says. He walks back toward the couple. For a moment Elly thinks they look familiar, but looks away quickly to gather her reality around her. Was this a fainting spell? Wasn't I just talking to Rochelle? What about Joseph? Pat? What day is this? She looks down at the table, at the blue notebook on car-washing habits.

She takes a sip of her hot coffee and breathes out. Again, she glances up at the couple at the counter and sees at least a dozen pierced body parts between them. She also sees why she thought she recognized them.

Elly shakes her head and smiles to herself as she watches Pat and the dark-haired woman leave the café carrying their double-tall mochas in paper cups.

Single White Female

I'M STANDING AT an old college friend's kitchen sink in Ojai washing strawberries that if you ask me don't need to be washed because they are so perfectly beautiful, red, and clean. I'm talking to my friend Sarah and her neighbor Willow. Willow wasn't invited to dinner, but she just showed up anyway. I'm a little peeved that I don't get Sarah and her family to myself, but I don't comment on it.

I will leave in the morning and drive my rented Geo Metro an hour on the picturesque, orange-grove-lined Highway 33 toward the Pacific. I'm a community relations associate at Brown and Caldwell, an environmental consulting firm in Seattle. They've asked me to attend a conference at the Holiday Inn in Ventura on how to get the public more involved in the decision-making process. Even though I should be flattered that they asked me to expand my expertise, I dread the idea of breaking up into small groups.

Sarah gave birth to Elena about fourteen months ago. I'd seen the pictures and heard the gurgles in the background on the telephone, and figured driving an hour out of my way was the least I could do to meet the child of one of my oldest friends. Besides, I hate staying alone in hotels.

Elena is spitting blue corn cereal all over her wooden high chair. Sarah is cutting up the chicken that will be added to the Tom Kah Gai and I'm telling her about Dana, my recent roommate from hell. Willow, who is slicing long stalks of lemongrass into two-inch pieces, is listening too. Even though I believe they're both rapt, I decide to make the story even more dramatic than reality needs it to be, because in reality it was pretty dramatic having Dana for a roommate.

I met Dana because I was invited to my cousin Simon's fiancée's bridal shower, the one I was two hours late getting to because my cousin Jennifer and I left late from Palm Springs, where I went with her and her friends for the weekend. I'd protested and did not want to go—who goes to the desert in the summer? She said it would be good for me since I was a lonely and pathetic mess. It'd been three years since my last real relationship, if you can call it that, and I think it showed in the very way I walked.

We were late to the shower, but there was plenty of food to be picked over, like fruit salad with kiwi and pineapple, and salmon mousse—untouched by human hands. I ate the mousse because I like it and because I'm from the Northwest and salmon is kind of like a state flag to us there.

As I munched on a cracker smeared with pureed fish, I saw a woman wearing a tasteful, Audrey Hepburn–ish black hat that I found myself coveting from across the room. She was alone and looked vaguely uncomfortable. I went over and introduced myself. Christine knew only the bride-to-be and not even that well. I liked her hat, so I continued our conversation about air and television and golf and other pleasantly limp topics.

Along the way it came out that her little sister had just moved to my hometown of Seattle and she thought it would be fabulous if I were to call her and you know, become her new best friend.

Calling Dana was my first mistake. My next mistake was giving her my address. At first she charmed me. She was sweet and unassuming and had blue eyes, all those traits I longed to possess. We sat at a bar in Fremont and drank beer and shared a plate of overpriced cheese and grilled red peppers and crunchy bread and hummus. The next thing I knew it was a week later and Dana and I were sitting in her car driving around Seattle neighborhoods looking for a house to live in together. We found a small bungalow across the street from Puget Sound in West Seattle and moved in. It was great at first, but eventually things turned really bad between us.

• • •

Ojai is awash with orange groves, and with all the windows open in Sarah's house I can almost smell the citrus on the dry wind. Sarah's husband, Eddie, walks in the door and hugs me even though I am still in the middle of telling my Dana story. He pulls Elena out of the high chair, opens the refrigerator, and offers Willow and me a beer. I take a swig of the cold yeasty brew. Then I measure out four tablespoons of fish sauce and two tablespoons of lime juice and pour the liquids into a large pot of chicken broth. Willow says she needs to run home and feed her ferret, Dodge.

Dana was invited to a party on an island in the San Juans and she brought me along because that's what new roommates do before things turn sour between them. There were sailboats and kayaks for everyone to use and oysters and crab for every-one to eat. I ate and paddled and I met Kevin and figured he was probably too gorgeous for me. It's not as if I'm one of those insecure females who thinks men are God's gift to us and we should be happy when any of them looks our way. No, it wasn't like that. This one was different. This one was an island all his own, a country to be conquered, a people to be taken hostage. Damn him.

It turned out he thought I was pretty cute too. Within a week we were making love and playing pool and hiking around the mountains where he lived in his cozy snow-surrounded A-frame. We cooked rice and changed the sheets and made love again. My friend Rochelle said I was obsessing because I no longer cared about anything in my life other than him or maybe because I stayed by the telephone waiting for him to invite me to drive the fifty miles to come visit him.

Two weeks went by and I told him I loved him even though I had no idea what he thought about at night or during the day or when he was in the shower, or even if he did think about anything other than snow and skiing down mountains covered with it. It didn't matter. All I knew was that having sex with him was like nestling with a rare white tiger cub: it had its dangers, but the smells, the touch, the smoothness of the skin, the roughness, the sweat, the strokes . . . I've strayed from the baby tiger analogy.

Thirty days passed, a landmark, and I wrote him:

Kevin,

I spent some time writing in my journal about you tonight. I hope someday I can let you read what I wrote and we can both smile at my foresight.

It was really nice that you called last night, drunk as you were. You so often say the absolutely perfect words to me and God, how you make me sigh. Love rushes. All of that mushy movie-lore stuff that I thought I would never feel as sincerely as I do with you and your looks and your smile and your hands oh yes your hands on my skin all of my skin and your mouth on my mouth and everywhere else it finds itself and your laugh the sort of laugh I could never get tired of hearing the kind of laugh that wriggles in between my toes when you laugh it and your voice so deep and strong and when you moan when you're next to me on top of me inside of me those sounds make me want more of you than I think you can give and your sweet tasting sweet smelling skin I want to lick you all over all the time and . . . you. Just you. All of you.

I can't help myself. I don't think I like our times apart very much. I'm hoping they don't come around too often.

Snow and quiet and a blazing fire inside a mountain cabin. Making love for 3 days and 3 nights. When can we do it again?

I just ate some lentil stew leftovers. I love cooking for you and I love that you cook for me. I have really sappy daydreams of us cooking together for family and friends.

Anyway, you're going to be reading this letter Friday the 12th, so here goes:

Happy One-Month Anniversary Darling

It was a nice one. Maybe I could talk you into a few thousand more? See you tonight.

Elly

But a few weeks later we got into a stupid fight and when he pulled up in front of my house, where Dana had been living before she got evicted, he told me to get out of the truck and I said no. He started driving away with me screaming and again he said to get out, but this time he reached around my back. Like an idiot I thought, Oh good, he's going to pull me close to him and apologize for being such a jealous and crazed man just because I had one beer with my ex-boyfriend Neil. But instead, he opened my door and gave me the littlest nudge out the door. Okay, he wasn't driving a million miles an hour, but I did lose my footing and I fell to the ground and split my chin open. I wrote him a letter begging for his forgiveness. I wondered where it was I went wrong and how it was I could win him back.

Kevin,

It was only days ago when we were tromping around in the snow on the land you bought. You pointing to the places where you would build your home. Me thinking to myself how happy I would be living there with you, raising a family, making love in the snow, drinking coffee on the deck.

It was only days ago when you spoke of us going off to New Zealand together.

It was only a few weeks ago that you told me you loved me.

It was only days ago that we made love in your bed. I remember the way your eyes looked down into mine.

It was only days ago that you were holding me and you asked me if I had any idea how much you cared for me. I said no. You fell silent.

It was two months ago that you insisted there was no way I would ever fall in love with you, and that I would break your heart.

How ironic.

A week ago we had a fight. I've replayed the scene over and over in my head and I still don't know what happened that night. You were so angry at me. What did we say to each other that brought out such tensions? I remember you telling me that you weren't ready for a relationship. More irony—wasn't it me who insisted that you should not get involved with anyone for a while? I should have listened to my own advice and been more patient.

I know my life has never been more unsettling since moving in with Dana. I downplayed my depression when I was with you, but I know my anxieties about living with her, along with job stress, flowed over into our friendship. For this I am truly sorry. But the frustration over not having this resolved in my own head is overwhelming to me. Sure, things were tough between us at times, really tough. But I was never more willing to work hard at changing the way I interacted in a relationship. Some things take time and effort, but I felt we were worth it. I thought, for a time, you did too.

Last week I called to tell you I missed you and wanted to try to be friends again, but you said I was no longer relevant to you and you hung up. How can that be so? How can it be that I can feel so broken inside, like my heart is on fire? I think of all those moments we spent together, those wonderful moments tucked inside all the other ones, and I feel lost in sadness. Holding your hand on the beach, taking River for a walk in the wind, flirting with you in pool halls, putting perfume on new places around my body and knowing you'd find them, meeting your friends, making love, God, making love with you, telephone calls that made everything better because you "weren't going anywhere," dinners in front of the television, crying on your shoulder in the movie theater, sharing our intimate memories and dreams, listening to dead '70s rock and roll stars, kissing you the first time on the park bench, watching you stand naked in your kitchen making your lunch, believing all the time we would make things work because it felt so right being with you.

I wish you success in all you pursue and I hope this letter finds you healthy and happy. Thanks again for letting me use the binoculars for a while. It's amazing what crows and whales and snow-peaked hills look like up close. I hope the Borneo book makes you smile and yearn for exploring the world's secret places the way it did for me. Take care,

Elly

He responded two months later with:

Elly,

It's taken me awhile to be able to write you. Wanted to . . . but also wanted to speak clearly. And I've been working 70–80 hours a week. [Poor dear.]

I'm not happy about the way things turned out. Felt so safe at first, then worried, finally very down. [Yeah, tell that to my busted chin, buster.]

I didn't think, I suppose. Imagined I'd made my intentions, my mindset, my paranoia very clear. Once bitten, twice shy.

Told myself and you many times, no fouls, no hurting, no push. [He should have thought twice about using that word, eh?] I have to have my safety. [His safety? Please.] I have to be able to say enough, time-out, this hurts. I have to respect when someone says "I can't" and give space asked for. Have to have that same space.

Life is for a long time and no instant, no "now" is important enough to make someone take part in a dance or ritual.

I can't do scenes. When I need to stop, it's for me.

When I need time . . . to think, that must be supported.

I was once in a place when "scenes" were common, no thought to when or where, public displays. Wanting to be alone not allowed. I will never be there again.

You and I had many differences, most were minor. I like myself casual, mostly. *GQ* occasionally. Want to be clean and attractive but don't care if I'm current. [What, like I did? Is this guy a martyr or what?] I like to think, but like to work hard too, just for work's own sake. I need a comfort zone, a way of life with space and safety and exits. [Like the door of a Chevy pickup.] Some people are bored with consistency. For me the more, the better.

Told you I was bothered by the concept of "I love you" before enough time is taken to say "I care." When I say you don't know me, respect would dictate belief.

What it finally came down to is that you were controlling the pace. [Me?] My heart, my feelings, seemed to me to be a minor issue and the ability for me to be heard and understood seemed only to get in the way of what you wanted.

Guess it was all probably less so than I feel. But then everything was done, weighed, by multiples. The Elly factor [My mother came up with that; so I exaggerate a tad now and then. So shoot me.] proved to be something I couldn't really relate to, it's not a part of me.

I am okay on my own. I like myself and also the direction I'm going. I have no problem with taking my time . . . both in my decisions and in relationships. I know I'll fall in love. And that it will be good. [I only hope for her sake it is.] In the meantime I'll live my life trying to grow, working toward goals I choose. Hope to also share that someday without losing myself.

For now, I need my space. Not going to share it, and ask no one's permission. I won't again make the mistake that someone is safe. I won't date, or spend casual time, until I'm ready.

I hope the rest of your life is falling back into place with you working for what you want. I know you'll get that. [Bless him.]

I'm returning books and photos, thanks for the loan. Please send my key [His key? Did he really think I put it on a chain around my neck for safekeeping?] ASAP and binocs when you can.

Kevin

Eddie puts on a Van Morrison cassette and we all sing along to "Brown Eyed Girl." The chicken and lemongrass and chili paste are simmering in the coconut milk and broth. Sarah suggests we go outside, so she picks up Elena and we all sit on the deck and listen to the creek flow by. The Ojai sky is streaked with reddish-orange clouds and I can see a fig tree in the waning light to my left. I am disappointed that there is no fruit on it.

At least by the time Kevin broke my heart, the roommate from hell was gone. She came along when I thought I needed a girlfriend. The kind that goes shopping and out to lunch with you. Who tells you no, your butt doesn't look big in those pants. I thought it would be good to have a friend like that. I thought when I was fifteen that marijuana made me smarter too.

Dana turned out to be nothing more than a big pain in my ass. During the first month living together she set up a personal face sauna on the dining room table, only inches from where I worked in the mornings at my computer. Picture it—the sound of the hissing steam, her face tucked into the plastic cup, her arms out to the sides.

She lived on unemployment and made it clear that she had no intention of finding a job because she made just enough to pay her share of the rent and the $400 car payment for her cool RX7. I guess that car of hers made her feel sexy, because she drove it fast and furious and maybe they do that in New Hampshire and guys think you're way bitchin' cruising in your gunmetal Mazda, but I was living in the great Northwest, where a good pair of Merrell hiking boots from REI would be the thing to turn heads.

I started helping her out a little each month, I'm not sure why. I got a nice raise at work and felt bad for her that she couldn't go out to the movies or lunch. We sometimes went food shopping together and I hated to see her sulk as we walked by the ice cream freezer. During those early days I didn't think buying her some Ben & Jerry's Chunky Monkey was such a big deal.

After a few months I started to feel a little taken advantage of, a little put out. She borrowed my clothes just to sit around giving herself those loud saunas, while her fat black cat pooped in the hallway. She left her dishes piled high in the stained porcelain sink (Dana did, not her cat). Even though we initially agreed that the television wouldn't be on during the day, she took to watching soap operas with the volume turned way down. It was hard to ignore the muffled sexual encounters in the next room. She threw dinner parties at a moment's notice. She served food from my side of the refrigerator and always forgot to recycle the beer bottles.

Fed up, I conspired with the landlady, Ellen, whom I once baby-sat for. She wanted to attend some home-based basket-making conference downtown and asked if I would mind watching her four-year-old twins, Madison and Laurel. Dana was out at a Mariners game, so the girls and I sat on the floor for three hours and played with my stuffed animal collection. I never let them play with Ed, though.

I got Ed when I was seven and wandering around a fog-encased twilight on the splintery boardwalk on the Jersey shore. I had this quarter burning a hole in my pocket and boy did I want to win one of those cuddly brown bears. The wheel at the concession stand had to land on the name of the square where you put the last quarter your father gave you before telling you to get lost, he's tired of hearing it already. I put my quarter on a square that had the name SAM on it, for no reason other than I didn't know anyone by that name, so it didn't have any connotations, good or bad.

The guy behind the counter spun the wheel and smiled at me like an impatient pedophile and asked me a couple of questions, but I ignored him. I was too busy focusing my squinted eyes on that wheel behind him, willing that darn wheel to land on SAM, SAM, SAM. The clicking of the wheel slowed as my heart quickened and it stopped on DAD. I pouted softly and turned to leave, but that pockmarked teenager said to my back, "Hey kid, you won."

I turned around to look and that wheel had miraculously changed and the shiny pointer was pointing to none other than SAM. I couldn't believe my eyes! I had won. That fellow smiled proudly at me, like I was his kid and I just brought home a report card brimming with A's in every subject. He pointed to the stuffed menagerie hanging on the walls and said, "Take yer pick, little lady."

I picked a brown bear that looked like he'd be a fine companion for getting me through those long dark nights when my mother and father were at some party or another and I knew the baby-sitter was too stoned to kill any monsters that might perchance attack me from under the bed. I hugged that bear to my chest and turned to walk away a second time, and a second time that guy called out to me. This time I wasn't sure if I should turn around or not. Did he suddenly have second thoughts? Was he going to make me give the bear back? I kept my back to him and slowly inched my way toward the Atlantic Ocean, but he yelled out to me, "Whatcha gonna name that bear of yours, princess?"

Easy. I turned back and smiled. I asked him his name. "Ed," he told me and wanted to know why I asked. I told him I'm naming my new bear after him, that's why.

Out of politeness, I wait to continue my Dana the awful roommate story until Willow comes back. She returns after a half hour with Rudy, a guy who is living on her property in his van. Rudy says the food smells great and Sarah invites him to join us for a bowl of the Thai coconut soup. Elena sits on my lap and pulls at my hair. She is a beautiful child and for a moment I think I want to move to Ojai and live out of my Toyota Tercel.

Dana started smoking cigarettes in the house and I asked her nicely to please smoke outside.

"You are on my case about everything these days," she responded. "Why don't you mind your own business."

Dying of secondhand smoke *was* my business. Keeping my sanity was, as well. "The lease says it's a no smoking house." I tried to be patient.

"I pay half the rent here, so half the oxygen is mine to use up."

"Whoa!" I couldn't believe her tone of voice, her aggression. "What's going on, Dana? I know we're not getting along that well, but the least we can do is compromise on some things. Smoking is totally out of line and you know it."

Dana turned her attention back to the television. An older woman in a pink negligee had her hands on her hips. She was telling some blonde in a black business suit that the blonde's husband was in her bed in the other room and if she were smart she'd just let him stay there.

"Dana," I repeated. "We should talk about splitting up, one of us moving out." My underarms were sweating.

She stubbed out her cigarette, petted her cat, Stinky, who was sitting on the windowsill beside her, and said, "I've got plenty of friends who would move in here and take your place."

I wanted to stay in the house. It was too beautiful to leave. Outside my window giant birds performed graceful dances; herons floated silently over the sea and pelicans dove dramatically into the surf. It was a symphony of acrobatics. Plus the backyard had a nice gazebo. "Dana. I want to stay. I can afford the whole rent by myself, so I don't even have to find a housemate."

"That's good, because it's not easy to live with you."

"And you think you're easy?" I countered. "Please move, Dana. Let's just get on with our lives."

She sighed, obviously impatient with my struggle to resolve the situation. "Okay, let's. I'm staying. Fuck off."

I called Ellen the next day. She was sympathetic. We came up with a Master Plan involving me not paying my share. Since both my name and Dana's were on the lease, we were both responsible. The plan was to have us both evicted, then re-rent to me only. So I didn't pay my half, and the landlady's husband, a nice guy named Bill who manages a furniture store and has gout, came over early on the fifth day of the month. He stood in the living room, looked at the two of us, and asked, "Where's the rest of the rent?" Dana pushed her furry eyebrows together like the sun was in her eyes and said she paid her share. Then she looked at me. I said that I didn't pay my share because I planned on moving out and needed the money for the other place's rent. Bill shook his head and made one of those TSK TSK sounds and finally said, "Well, one of you has to come up with the full rent by tonight or you're both going to be evicted."

Dana stood there, a look of disbelief washed across her pinched little face. Bill started leaving, being done with his part of the secret plan, and Dana said to him, "Bill, I think you should know that I have a police report on Elly." Bill asked, "What for?" And she said, all dramatic like, like she'd been holding this valuable little tidbit in the back of her tiny head for sometime, "Because Elly has threatened to kill me with a knife while I sleep."

What? Sure I once said that it was too bad she was alive and that she took up space in my house, but I never said I wanted to kill her with a knife. If I had gone off the deep end and done something irrational, I would've chosen a neater way, like slipping her some sleeping pills, not that that's necessarily neat. You can take a lot of sleeping pills or sedatives and not die. My brother did that when he was seventeen and sad because some girl wouldn't go out with him or because my father didn't love him enough.

He took all the Valium my mom had in her medicine chest and tried to die. I came home from one of my friends' houses on a Saturday night and as I walked up the stairs to my bedroom, I saw the bathroom light on and the door open. On the landing I reached out to look past the door of the bathroom and I saw just enough smeared feces out of the corner of my right eye to know that I didn't want to open that door any more than it was open. I went to my room next to the bathroom. Mine was the one that had red stained glass in the window shutters, so that when the sunshine hit it during midafternoon, the room glowed with a little girl pink hue, while my older brother, the one who had just eaten all those pink Valium pills, had blue glass. My younger brother had golden windows. The golden child.

I walked to my little girl pink room with pink carpeting and a pink telephone and pink stuffed animals and pink bed-cover (none of this was the result of the sun coming through and washing everything with pink light, because it was night-time). I found my brother lying atop my pink bed, curled in a fetal position and moaning. I, being the polite and caring fifteen-year-old sister that I was, screamed at him to get off my bed. He looked up, startled to see me there, or maybe just startled to still be alive, mumbled, "Sorry," slithered off my bed, and headed down the hallway to his room. I wasn't a rocket scientist, but I put two and two together, what with the shit in the bathroom and my brother disoriented enough to be in my room, where he was not, and never had been, per-mitted. I walked slowly down to his room, which wasn't glowing blue at this point because it was night, and I asked him if he was okay, and did he need anything. His eyes were closed and there was sweat on his face and his clothes weren't tucked in. I wished Mom and Dad were home so I didn't have to deal with this on my own and just as I thought this, the front door opened downstairs and my parents' slightly tipsy voices wafted up the stairs. I greeted them on the landing and detoured them toward the bathroom, where my father screamed, upon seeing the floor, "What the hell's going on here?"

Before I could say anything, they raced down to my brother's room. They got him to admit taking the Valium and my mother reacted in her typical dramatic fashion and put her hand to her heart as my father called the ambulance and they all left for the hospital. My baby brother and I had to go across the street and stay with the Sullivans, who were nice enough, but we had to eat dinner there the next day. I still to this day resent my brother for making me eat Stove-Top stuffing and baked ham.

I wouldn't have killed Dana that way. I wouldn't have killed her at all. I don't know why she said that. She was selfish, psychotic, and a liar, but still I felt hurt by the accusation. I got hurt a lot that year. First by her. Then by Kevin. It was a shitty year, now that I think of it.

We all sit around the pine dining table and I place my tie-dyed purple and blue napkin across my lap. Sarah ladles the Tom Kah Gai into carved wooden bowls. Rudy passes me a bowl of chopped cilantro to sprinkle across the steaming soup.

Willow asks me to continue the story about my crazy roommate. I shift in my seat and know that even though everyone is slurping the pungent stew, their eyes are on me. I want to be interesting. To drive the point home I decide to ask them if they ever saw *Single White Female*, referring to the horror movie about a girl (Bridget Fonda) who lets another girl

(Jennifer Jason Leigh) move in with her after her boyfriend dumps her. You think at first they're going to have fun and get along and borrow each other's clothes and go to movies together, but it turns out that the new roommate is really crazy. She thinks she killed her twin at birth and now that gives her an excuse to look like the other roommate. She steals her mail (and her male and gives him head—a great fellatio scene), and dyes her hair to match her new friend.

I could go on, but that would give the movie away. You may want to rent it one day when you're in the video store and you're broke and scanning the ninety-nine-cent wall where the old but still watchable videos sit. You're hoping that there's one you haven't yet seen and there it is, *Single White Female*, but you think, "I can't watch this, I already know what happens at the end."

I feel it wise to use this movie as a kind of allegory to describe what I experienced living with my own mad roommate from New Hampshire. I look at Sarah across the table midway through a sentence and I ask, "Have you ever seen *Single White Female*?" and before she answers, Willow, the one who wasn't really invited, looks up from her spoon and says, "You lived with Bridget Fonda?"

SWM

SHE CIRCLES:

ONLY THE BEST But not the egotistical. Confident yet humble. That's what I aim for and that's what I have to offer, in all respects: looks, personality, character. For sincere friendship and whatever else that may happen. I'm late 20s, SWM, athletic, successfully self-employed (very) and having loads of fun. I love the Northwest and fully enjoy all its virtues. Business takes me far and away quite often but the best part is always coming home. I'm degreed but does it matter? 6 feet tall (with my boots), dark and handsome (very). I feel extremely lucky to live and experience an era that I think will be the best yet for (most of) mankind, the Technology and Information Age. Overwhelming, and yet so power-

fully productive and beneficial. My kind of
Age. Please send photo with reply.

She writes:

Dear Mr. Only the Best,

So, you are in your late 20s and confident about
your looks and your personality. I like that in a man.
In fact, your ad was the only one not to ask for any
particular traits in a woman. Refreshing, or just self-
absorbed? You can let me know. Your last bit in the
ad? What are you talking about? Do you sleep with
your modem? Are you an e-mail junkie? Do tell.

Anyway I'm fourteen years old and my friend,
Nancy Day (her real name is Dawn, but for obvious
reasons, she preferred to be called Nancy), is in love
with a guy named Billy. When at last he asks her out
on a date she is ecstatic, grabbing me in the high
school cafeteria, hysterical with triumph.

On Friday, she tells me that Billy's friend Beaver
is coming to town and unless she could fix him up
with a date, their date was off. She begged. What could
a best friend do? I mean, wasn't it Nancy who helped
me through my trauma when my boyfriend Butch was
sent to juvenile hall for stealing an opal ring to give
to me? But Beaver? What does he have, buck teeth, I
ask? She insists he is probably a really nice guy because

any friend of Billy's . . . (Not that Billy was a bur-
geoning high school hero or anything.)

The doorbell rang at 7:00 on Saturday. When I
opened the door, only Nancy and Billy stood on the
threshold. I looked past their shoulders toward the
car parked out front with a questioning frown on my
face. Before I could utter a word, Nancy said, "Tell
your parents that Billy is your date. If they meet Beaver they won't let you out."

My parents came downstairs to meet my evening
date. I felt only slightly guilty about lying to them about
Billy being Beaver, but my guilt was overshadowed by
the image of what was awaiting me in the car.

Needless to say Beaver had buck teeth. But they
were less noticeable than his black greasy hair trapped
under a hairnet. Beaver was a gang-banging Chicano
from East Los Angeles.

We went to a drive-in movie. I paid for all four of
us. Nancy and Billy made out in the back and I spent
that glorious evening fighting to keep Beaver's hands
off me.

Suffice to say, that was my one and only blind date.
If I were the sort of gal who believed in setting prec-
edents, I would not be writing this letter to you, but
hey, I've got an open mind.

Me: Hmmm . . . I've never done this before, so
what do I say? All the ads seem to say what people's
friends think about them ("My friends say I'm attrac-

tive; My friends say I'm smart"). What a load of shit. Who really cares what your friends say about you? They are your friends, after all, and true friendship should be unconditional friendship, or it is only fleeting.

Okay, I've segued away from the issue here. Me. Well, I'm early 30s, and work toward making the planet a better place. I'm 5' 6" and weigh about 118 lbs. I don't own a scale. Brown hair. Brown eyes. I look good in a mini skirt but prefer to wear 501s. Yeah, yeah, you could say I'm pretty. It just kinda curdles my skin a little to write it.

I'm educated, well-traveled, and well-read. My favorite fruit is the Fuyu persimmon. Give me a break here. Am I doing this the right way??? I adore courtship (flowers, dinners, walks), but my grandmother keeps telling me she doesn't want to die without seeing me happily married (no pressure there).

I'm a bit of a dilettante. I do many things and excel at a few. I was kicked out of Girl Scouts because I grabbed my friend during a hike and took her on my own tour. Upon returning to the trailhead, we were greeted by policemen and parents. I did not earn a medal for cross-country exploration. I was thrown out of modeling school at age thirteen because a woman sat me in a chair and began plucking out my eyebrows. I said, "What the fuck do you think you're doing?" My courses were terminated due to "manners unbecoming a lady." I've grown up to be a fine lady and appreciate being treated as one. Just stay away from my eyebrows.

Enough. Just write me back and we can talk more. I'm not enclosing a picture. Don't worry, I'm pretty.

Elly

First Date: Ryan. Who names a half-Chinese kid Ryan? He is definitely handsome and tall in his expensive leather boots, if a bit on the scrawny side. Mom is Chinese. Dad is out of the picture, but obviously Occidental. Black hair and brown eyes, with that ever-so-slight epicanthal fold revealing his heritage. Ryan owns a land development company and thus goes around developing land, mostly in undeveloped countries south of the border. Not going to be any environmental hero anytime soon. The computer perversion? She never did find out. They went to a Spanish place, shared some lousy tapas. Who the hell came up with this tapas idea? Overpriced morsels on a Spanish-style plate. A spatter of spicy mussels here. Some oily meat there. Can't fill up on the stuff unless you are a millionaire. She did not want to whine about being hungry, so she just ate a frozen burrito when she got home. He bragged about his hot tub and 50-inch television screen. Checked his watch a lot, and never did look her straight in the eye. Said he had a great time and would call her. Yeah. Or sell her the Brooklyn Bridge at a really good price.

Second Date: Who would have thought? He called and she accepted. They went for Mexican this time. She did not have to leave hungry; she had the supremely filled burrito and he the tostada, a girl's lunch dish. When she picked a strand of shredded lettuce from the top of the heap of beans and tomatoes and boiled chicken, he giggled like she had just leaned over the table and planted a hickey on his neck. So much for the confident playboy. He was beginning to look at her when she talked too.

He is cute and she thinks children of mixed race are ineffably adorable. But, marriage with Ryan? She thinks not. Maybe a short affair. Or possibly joining him on one of his reconnaissance trips when he checks out potential countries to savage.

Date Three: Never happened. He walked her to her door post-burrito and kissed her. *Disgusting,* as her friend Gaye used to say as she turned up her nose at such things as fried fish and beer bellies. He sopped her chin with saliva. That was not enough to dissuade her entirely, but when he pushed his hand up inside her shirt and got a quick hard squeeze out of one of her breasts, she knew he was too young for her. Too undeveloped. She found herself looking at her own watch when he tried to talk her into another get-together. Nice, but no cigar. Oh well, who's next?

She circles:

WOMANIZING DRUNK NEEDS JOB
Bright, attractive, professional, fit (phys,

**emotional, and $), SWM with HAIR! I'm
6'3", 35, & enjoy life's diversity. If you're 25–
35, FUN & HAPPY, with the same qualities,
RESPOND or live with the burden of yet another missed opportunity. "Babes" with
brains ONLY.**

She writes:

Dear Womanizing Drunkard,

Enclosed please find one pair of plastic glasses with
nose and moustache attached. Wear them when we
meet or I will never be able to tell you apart from all
the other womanizing drunks out there.

Anyway I'm fourteen years old and my friend, Nancy
Day (her real name is Dawn, but for obvious reasons,
she preferred to be called Nancy), is in love . . .

Elly

He was attractive on the telephone. Sexy deep twang.
Worried if she might be turned off by his three-year-old son
from a previous marriage. (He should have written DWM—the
D being for Divorced—instead of SWM, but the rules governing
singles' ads are just asking to be broken.) A vice president of
a major savings and loan. When she learned about the job, she
figured he was safe enough (see: "mature") to give him a go.

They met at a downtown steakhouse. He claimed he

loved the plastic nose-attached glasses but refused to wear them. When she got there, though, wearing a tight black skirt and flowered blouse and heels, she knew who he was by the sound of his booming Southern accent. He was sitting at the bar flirting with two women. He saw her and gave her the once-over. Until she actually convinced him she was his date for the night, she guessed he would have just gone right back to those two gin and tonic—slurping babes.

Very tall, slightly rotund body, like muscles taking a breather, splendidly rich brown wavy hair and excellent wool suit. They sat in a wooden booth, dark mahogany adding appropriately to the steakhouse aura. Closed in and at last face-to-face. Banker, yes, George Bailey, no. Not even close. Condo owner. Loved to drink. Stared at her breasts while she ordered a nice halibut steak topped with a citrus salsa.

Right after ordering she got up to go to the bathroom. She was gone long enough to pee, swish her hair up and down so it had body again, and head out. She got to the table and the food had already been served. No big deal except that he was eating. The pig. If the guy had been a gentleman in any other way she might have overlooked this obnoxious impatience on his part, but in the grand scheme of things he was just another bulbous-faced, dumbfounded boy who probably made love with his eyes closed.

He walked her to her car, told her he found her wildly

attractive, but when he leaned toward her face to register a kiss there, her head sprang back like the metal pull on a pinball machine. She squinted a smile at him, said, "I don't kiss on the first date," slammed the car door, locked it quickly, and drove off.

She circles:

> **TALL SLENDER ATTRACTIVE SM 37, who delights in defying stereotypes, seeks insightful, attractive SF, 30–40, for hiking, off-beat films and music, exchanging affection. Must enjoy simple quiet.**

She writes:

> Dear Mr. Tall, Slender, Attractive SM who delights in defying stereotypes,
>
> So, you're into off-beat films. Ever see *Santa Sangria*? Daunting. And if I may be so bold as to ask, what, pray tell, is "simple quiet"? As opposed to complex quiet where it is difficult to say nothing to your companion? Who was it that said, "True friendship means never having to say anything at all"? Maybe I said it.

Anyway I'm fourteen years old and my friend, Nancy
Day (her real name is Dawn, but for obvious reasons,
she preferred to be called Nancy), is in love . . .

Elly

She agreed to meet him at a downtown art museum after he
was sweet enough to send her some guitar strings in the mail.
He told her on the telephone that he loves music. She told
him she had a folk guitar that was never played because the E
string was broken and she didn't have enough motivation to
replace it.

The theme of the exhibit was "Sexual Inhibitions."
Gary was a wee bit more into the painfully immature expres-
sions of tied-up emotions than she. He took his time staring
into each cubby's ridiculous displays and she stared at him. A
beauty that man. Like a ski standing upright, he is long and
sleek and colorful. Blond hair flopping over his tiny round
gold-rimmed glasses. A disheveled flannel shirt hardly tucked
into a pair of baggy blue jeans never looked so sexy.

At lunch in a nearby Indian restaurant, he seemed pre-
occupied with the artwork of that morning. Over a bland
chicken curry he attempted to deconstruct the vision of artisans
who she felt had little insight. "What do you think that one
woman was saying, with that multicolored rope tied around a
Pepsi can?"

"Maybe she equates sexual need with thirst." She wanted to laugh. Who cares? she thought to herself. But he is awfully darling to look at. And those hands of his. Fingers like stretched-out taffy melting on an Atlantic City boardwalk. She drank chai while imagining those fingers strumming her belly.

They talked on the telephone four times that week, and she learned about his childhood in Nebraska, the sixth of nine children. Fervent Catholics, the rest of the clan was still living in the Midwest, but he escaped after school to the Emerald City in the cold Northwest. The only negative was his job status: unemployed librarian. "Hard to get work at one of the branches. Lots of competition," he had said.

They met for a walk around Myrtle Edwards Park. The sun hid behind thick clouds, but just knowing it was there, lurking, kept the day warming itself. He took her hand and she allowed him. Her neck started hurting from looking up at him while he was talking, so she just let her eyes wander past the grain elevator across the horizon of Puget Sound. Oddly, the air smelled like pine trees.

A few weeks later she met her buddy John at Pike Place Market, where they each walked with a falafel stuck in their fists. Gooey tahini sauce ran down her wrist and she licked it off after taking a bite of the warm crunchy garbanzo ball.

"Tell me about this new guy," John demanded after he

threw the pita crust and half a dozen napkins in the trash. They sat on the cold cement wall behind the Market and leaned their elbows into the damp grass. They scanned the Sound before them, dodging the drunks who wheezed by them, bent-over shapes zigzagging the vista.

"He's tall and gentle and only slightly funny. Which is too bad since he's so damn good-looking. Where's the perfect man, I ask you?"

"Sitting right here next to you, sweetheart."

She ignored him and sighed as she bit into the apple she had tucked into her coat pocket on the way out the door that morning.

"Had sex yet?"

"No. We can't. What I mean is, there's this other thing," she said.

He looked at the side of her face. "What other thing?"

"Well. See. He has this problem and he's in therapy for it. Took him two weeks to finally tell me, but I totally respect him for being so up front about it." She started twirling her hair with her fingers. "He's into exposing himself to women."

"What?!" John was up on his feet now and looking down at her. "He's a pervert?"

"Call it what you want, but he's getting help for it. He just really likes to have people see him naked, is all. It's not like he's ever touched anyone. He's not a rapist, for Christ's sake."

John insisted, "Tell me more."

"Now you're making me feel weird about this and I was okay about it. Shit." She picked at a pimple that was forming on the right side of her neck. "He exposes himself. Period. Only he made the mistake of doing it just outside of the Ravenna library, where he worked. The woman he exposed himself to screamed. You can't blame her. Usually he just gets in his car and drives off before he gets caught. He said he always wore some kind of disguise so no one could ever identify him, but this time a cop just happened to be driving by."

"Good thing."

"So, he got arrested and, of course, fired from his job, since his boss came out to see what all the ruckus was about. Now he's in therapy and his therapist told him not to get physically involved with anyone for at least a year."

John was nonplussed. "And you're going to continue seeing this creep?"

"You think it's a bad idea? I mean, he's really sweet and has been totally honest. I guess I don't think it's that horrible a crime. He just wants attention maybe."

John pulled her up toward him and held her arms tight. "If you ever see this guy again, I will kill you. Are you crazy? He's a deviant. End of story. You think it's some harm-

less prank, opening his coat and flapping his dick in the wind.
But I'll tell you this. He is sick in the head and the last thing
I need to be worrying about is him hurting you in some sick
way." He let go of her arms and shook his head. "Promise me
it's over. Promise me."

She knew in her heart that what John was saying
was right. The implications were too strange and it was not
like he was the perfect guy for her. She frowned her agree-
ment. "Promise. Scout's honor. Never again do I date the
deviant."

Done.

She circles:

> SW MENSCH, 31, creative, good-looking,
> sensitive, accomplished. Has just about every-
> thing except someone to share it with. I'm
> seeking a real companion, 22–33. NS, orig-
> inal, fit, adventurous. Photo appreciated.

She writes:

> Dear Mr. Mensch,
>
> So, you're good-looking, creative, sensitive and ac-
> complished. Accomplished at what? What do you cre-
> ate? So many questions.

Anyway I'm fourteen years old and my friend, Nancy Day (her real name is Dawn, but for obvious reasons, she preferred to be called Nancy), is in love . . .

                                                    Elly

He is hysterical on the telephone. East Coast origins. Well-educated. Big important computer guy at Nintendo. This guy had serious potential. Called her mom before the date.

"What should I wear?"

"You haven't asked me that question for ten years."

All day her imagination skipped down imaginary wedding aisles. She put on black tights, a red plaid skirt, black turtleneck sweater, and black medium-heeled shoes. Perfume between her small breasts. Plenty of dousing room.

He rang her doorbell and she went outside to meet him. "Never let a new man come into your house," her mother had warned. "No matter how much you trust him." He held a bouquet of tulips and wore a shabby wool blazer over stained khaki pants. His shoes had seen better days. She told him to wait while she ran back in to put the flowers in water. As she opened her front door, he said, "Why don't you change your shoes, too. I'd like to walk to a restaurant."

"But it's raining. I'd really rather drive, if you don't mind."

He had a photograph of an older woman stuffed into

a fold on his dashboard. His dead mother, he confessed. They drove the few minutes in silence.

At the Queen City Grill they got a table in the back of the restaurant. The low wooden chairs were uncomfortable and she squirmed uneasily. "How about we share a Caesar Salad? They're to die for here."

"I hate sharing food."

She did not like this man. More to the point, he hated her. She could tell. So promising on the telephone, such a selfish dud in person.

"Mind if I have a martini?" she asked.

"Thought you didn't drink?" he said.

She replied, "I don't usually, but this might be a long meal."

"Go ahead. Do what you want," he said.

Is this guy at a funeral or a first date? Morose. Melancholy. Morbid. Maladjusted. She thought of all the *M* words that fit the moment. Malaise. Mismatched. She smiled.

"I think I'll have the crab cakes," he said, putting down the menu and looking at her. "I know they're probably going to be mostly bread crumbs. Can't for the life of me find a chef in this city who can make a good crab cake, you know?"

Mannequin. Mendacious. Meaningless. "Dahlia Lounge makes pretty good ones. Been there?" she asked, trying like a lion tamer to evoke some response from his drugged charge, if only to give the ticket holders their money's worth.

Two martinis later and he is almost charming in a disaffected way. She got him to drink a beer with his crab and bread crumb cakes. She made him smile with her story about her clumsy date with the flaccid banker. But he never bothered to relive the man he was on the telephone. Must have been a friend talking for him. That's it! Cyrano de Seattle. He obviously has a friend who makes the initial phone calls, lures them into his charming persona, then sends this guy on the loose and hopes the girl does not notice the difference. Mistrust. Misinformation. Messy. "Want to share dessert?"

"I've got to be honest with you." He looked down at his hands. Malignant. Miserable. Misfit. "I'd just as soon take you home and call it a night. You're not someone I care to spend any real time with. Nothing personal."

Mercy.

She circles:

ONE TIME BAD BOY 32 SWM, rebellious and complex. Tall, good-looking, highly educated, accomplished, seeks beautiful, intelligent, professionally successful, and adventurous woman 25–35 to stir my imagination, challenge me, and capture my heart. Photo apprec.

She writes:

Dear Mr. One Time Bad Boy,

So, you're looking for a spirited woman who has a rebellious nature and can stir your imagination. Easy. Challenge you? Not a problem. Capture your heart? All depends on what kind of cage it's behind or how dense a jungle it's lurking in.

Anyway I'm fourteen years old and my friend, Nancy Day (her real name is Dawn, but for obvious reasons, she preferred to be called Nancy), is in love . . .

Elly

They met at a jazz bar. He took time off from a busy caseload down at the public defender's office to meet her. He made it clear from the start he was doing her a favor. She named him rebound man and wished that she had long curly blonde hair and her name was Katie—the recent love of his life who left without a trace. Well, not really. More than a trace of despair seeped from his demeanor and voice. "Women are wicked," he pronounced during intermission. The music was bland and the shish kebab and salad vinaigrette they shared added little flavor.

Yet she was entranced. A New England philosopher with a keen intuition about people (not the wicked women

part). He told her how he had spent years working with troubled boys after growing out of his own troubled youth. A bad
home life sent him looking for self-worth with a bad crowd.
Small-time burglary and then drugs, it took the help of a "Big
Brother" to pull him out of the downward spiral. He left the
streets and hunkered down in the local library, discovering
Nietzsche, Kant, and other thinkers. He extended what he
learned toward volunteerism. His hard-won attitude and in-
exorable patience, he confessed modestly, made him extremely
successful at turning around the lives of vulnerable street kids.

     After a degree in psychology he moved to Seattle to a
more urban street setting, but lost his faith in the system when
he was stopped over and over again by bureaucracy.

     She stared into his green eyes as he told his story. A
hero, she thought. A bit righteous, but he is intelligent, so
comfortable with himself. And that shirt he is wearing; a hard-
ened chest pressed against the blue cotton fabric. She liked the
smell of his aftershave.

     They went to Lake Union after the show and sat on a
concrete retaining wall. Again he brought up Katie. She waited
for the moment to pass and politely inquired about whether
he would ever get over this woman. Surprisingly he said it
would probably take a long time. She thought that was too bad;
he was definitely a potential. Then he kissed her hard on the
mouth, holding her arm tightly with one hand, pulling her
closer to him with the other. "What about Katie? I don't think

it's such a good idea to get me involved with you if you're still in love with another woman."

"I've got some extra emotions floating around," he said. "Maybe you can help me get over her."

She liked him and was willing to give a few weeks of her time to excise the girl who wanted nothing more to do with him. He was too busy to get together but they talked on the telephone. Every conversation started out promising enough. He told her he thought about her, that he was excited by the newness of her. Inevitably, though, the conversation turned to Katie. "I saw her playing tennis on my way to work today. God, she looked so good. I almost went up to talk to her, but chickened out."

She comforted him. "Time will make her dissipate into thin air. I promise." She pictured his brown sandy hair and that first kiss. "Remember, I'm here for you if you need me." They hung up.

The weeks passed like this. Late-night phone calls. One lunch meeting on a park bench. Pleasant chat about work; Katie was unmentioned. A snail's pace romance with a leftover lover hanging like a storm cloud over them. "I'm going to visit my family in San Diego this weekend, just to let you know," she told him.

"How about if I meet you down there?"

"Really?" Her skin caught fire.

"Sure. It would be good to get away. I can take some

work and we can hang out on that perfect white sand beach you told me about."

She picked him up at the airport Saturday morning. All through Friday her mother sang skeptical songs. "You're wasting your time. He's still involved with another woman," she said while making the sandwiches for their picnic lunch.

He gave her a book of poetry. Tess Gallagher. A lover's lament over a dead husband. Perfect. Did he want her to feel like he did? They went to the beach and he rubbed lotion on her back. His hand on her warm skin soothed her. She felt like she did when she snuggled under her down comforter in the cold of winter. Ensconced in heat. She jumped in the ocean while he worked. When she emerged from the sea and shook her wet salty hair over him, he jumped. "What the hell did you do that for?" he screamed.

"Sorry. Thought it might be refreshing." She sat on the towel next to him.

"I hate people who have no sense of another person's space. Katie was so good at giving me time alone when I needed it."

She was undone. "Well, she's given you all the space in the world now, eh?"

"That was uncalled for."

"No. Your pining is uncalled for." She wiped the sand from her shoulder. "You came down here to be with me. Not her. You can't seem to go five minutes without talking about her or comparing me to her. You have got to grow up. Get over her."

He took off his sunglasses and wiped them on the bottom of his shorts. "I don't think I'm ready to be over her," he said. Then he turned away from her, put his head on his upturned palm, opened a manila file folder, and began reading.

She hugged him good-bye at the airport, a day earlier than planned. Not even a night spent together. That would have convinced him. She should have made him stay instead of giving in. Sex might have won him over.

She discovered—after she ran into him on the street four months later—that she would have made a grave mistake. She asked him how he was. He pouted and said, "Still in love with a phantom, I guess. You?"

She crumbles up the paper, stained red with circles. And throws it away.

The Other Side

"**WHY DO WE** have to go across the bridge just to look through other people's junk?" Richard asked Naomi as they buckled Brittany into her car seat. He was not up to a day of garage sales, what with all that work he had waiting for him back at his home office. At least eighty e-mails awaited his reply and damn if he wasn't behind on smoothing out the rough corners on the Century 21 Real Estate website.

Naomi turned down the visor and checked her teeth in the mirror. "You promised you'd take some time off and spend it with us this weekend. You worked last weekend. Just a couple of hours," she whined as she wiped a small undetectable lipstick smear from her right incisor. "Here, I have the paper. A few good ones in Queen Anne, then a quick hop onto 99 and over the West Seattle Bridge for two or three more."

"Do you have the map?" Richard asked, checking his speed on the digital display on the BMW's dash.

"You are amazing," Naomi said, shaking her blonde head. "You grew up here and you still don't know your way around the city."

"Cut me a break, babe. I grew up on the eastside. Not downtown. It wasn't like my family drove into the city all the time."

"Not even every now and then? You and your friends never felt like exploring Seattle, getting out of Bellevue and maybe adventuring a little?" Naomi leaned her head back on the headrest and sighed. She'd been living in the Seattle area for going on two years and already she knew the many neighborhoods that lined Puget Sound. She and Brittany often took the Lexus and crossed the great I-90 expanse that rode for miles over Lake Washington. She loved strolling her baby daughter along Queen Anne Avenue, stopping for a Cobb salad at the 5-Spot, buying bedtime stories at Queen Anne Books. Or venturing out to the University District, where she'd watch the young students bound down University Avenue on their way to class after a quick lunch at a tacqueria or noodle house. She, so close to the same age as they, and yet here she was, a wife and mother already. She'd browse the shelves in the University Book Shop, wistfully lost in travel book photographs. If there was an interesting reading she'd sit and listen, hoping Brittany's nap would last the course of the talk. It rarely did.

Her few friends, the wives of Richard's friends mostly, never went along. They were happy to roam the two hundred stores inside the Bellevue Square Mall. Even tennis was an indoor activity for these women. Rare but glorious Northwest sunshine would show up at their doorsteps and they would head to the club for exercise. Naomi suggested walks around the lake or a shopping expedition to the funky Wallingford neighborhood, but they fell on deaf ears, adorned as they were with large diamonds.

No, she didn't fit in very well. She knew she'd be starting over, moving to a Seattle suburb from her small community in California's Sierra foothills. Her hometown was a quiet village that teemed only on weekends when tourists from San Francisco wandered the tiny steep streets of the Gold Rush— era hamlet. Naomi grew up in a comfortable log home on twelve acres of pines, dark and musty in the winter, cool and sweet in the summer. Her father was a forestry consultant and her mother taught middle school. She and her brother spent their summer days in blazing sunshine exploring the ever-changing topography of the encircling mountains and swimming and playing along the boulder-strewn shores of the Yuba River.

When her father died on a snowy mountain road, her dreams of college died with him. She worked full-time for a year and when it looked like a four-year institution was financially out of the question, her mother insisted she enroll in the local junior college while they figured out how to make ends meet and pay for a university. She took a photography course and journalism courses, the two that were offered. She wanted to travel and write about other cultures, she told her mother, brother, and any co-workers, when they would listen.

Then she met Richard. He and two friends came to town to ride their mountain bikes along the hundreds of miles of roads and trails through the foothills, and farther east, into the mountains of Lake Tahoe. She was working at the local café when he walked in, dusty and hot.

"Hi. What's good here?" he asked, and whisked the sweat off his forehead with a dirty forearm. There was some black stubble forming on his chin and his T-shirt had a tear in the side.

"Depends on what you define as good," she countered with a smirk.

He looked at her and smiled, then he looked down at his knees and wiped one clean. He looked back up at her and she was staring at him. One of his friends smacked him on the back.

"C'mon already. Order."

"Uh. Hmm. Let me see." Richard looked at the chalkboard menu above Naomi's head. "I'll take a blackberry Italian soda and dinner with you tonight."

• • •

He took her to the French place where all the tourists go on Saturday nights. Naomi's parents had taken her there five years ago when it was called by another name, but still cost an arm and a leg. She was fifteen. She remembered when the waitress put the salmon down in front of her. The smell of the hot crispy fish, glistening with butter. A sprig of tarragon lay across the flesh so perfectly. She never imagined she'd ever be eating there again.

Richard didn't hesitate to order the grilled scallops for twenty-two dollars or a thirty-dollar bottle of wine. She rested her hands across her lap and was conscious of her posture. She stalled when the waitress asked her what she wanted.

"Please, Naomi. Don't look at the prices," Richard said softly, so the waitress wouldn't hear. "If you want to, order six different things and just take a bite of each. Money is not a concern."

After dinner Richard kissed her while standing in front of the restaurant, the taste of the wine still saturating his mouth. He told her he'd call her every day, and he did. Two months later she flew up to see his world. He wouldn't let her leave. When she protested, said she had bigger plans for her future, he promised her that she could take classes at the University of Washington. That they'd travel the world together.

They married four months later. She expected they would go on a lengthy honeymoon to some perfect place where you could sit on your deck and watch your dinner being caught and dragged in from the ocean a hundred feet from your suite.

"I'm sorry, sweetie. Not yet. I've got to grow the business first. It's not like it's my money," he said. "I owe the investors their due."

Three months later she missed her period.

Naomi leaned over, turned off the air-conditioning, and pressed the automatic window button. The smell of the leather bucket seats and baby powder made her queasy. "Turn right at Warren. There. 1420. Ick. Looks like a lot of junk, huh?"

"You dragged me out here. Let's at least get out and poke around," Richard said, unbuckling his seat belt. They wandered down the narrow aisles of used clothing splayed across the front lawn and headed to the garage, where, hopefully, the good stuff was. Ten other people wandered the front of the small green house, sided with aging asbestos shingles. Richard picked up a brass chandelier and tugged at a hanging wire. Naomi kicked open a dirty camping stove with her toe. Not likely to use this, she thought. During their short courtship Richard had talked enthusiastically about the Cascades, the many hiking trails leading to glacial lakes only a half hour drive from his house. She hated leaving her mountain refuge, but pines are pines everywhere. The smell of bark after a rain or the lull of a weakened waterfall trickling methodically over slippery rocks could be found in Washington's mountains too, she knew. But she and Richard had taken only one walk together: while she was pregnant with Brittany, they had climbed the famous Mount Si trail up through the clouds and peered down triumphantly over the town of North Bend. She was so happy that day and wanted more days like it.

"Let's go," Richard said, as disappointed as she was that no treasures were hidden beneath the discards. "Where to now, oh princess rubbish lover?"

They drove to six more garage sales, Naomi buying a few books and a lace tablecloth. Richard, collector of rock and roll albums, found his riches in a cardboard box in front of a West Seattle beach cottage. Over fifty used albums in their original covers for ten bucks. He smiled the whole way home.

October brought with it the beauty of an Indian summer. Gold and red leaves drifted down onto the blanket where Naomi sat in the warmth of a scented wind reading stories to Brittany. Richard came out of the back door and handed Naomi a battered notebook. "You remember when I bought those albums this summer?" he asked. "I don't think this was supposed to be in the box."

"You just got around to looking at those albums? We

bought them months ago." Naomi took the book and placed it for a moment on the blanket next to her gurgling squirming daughter.

"Yeah, well. I had some compiling to do and had an hour to kill so I—"

"Why didn't you kill it with us?" Naomi fretted and turned away, picking up the small red tattered loose-leaf book.

"Anyway, as I was saying. I started pulling out the albums and dusting them off and stuff and voilà, I see this in the box. I think it's someone's diary or something."

"I wonder if there was an ad in the Lost section of the newspaper. Have you noticed?"

"It's been over two months, Naomi. Have you been reading the Lost ads?"

"No, but I haven't lost anything. I guess I can take a ride back to that house in West Seattle where we got it from."

"Maybe there's a name in it. You look through it. I'm going back to work."

"How about a kiss for your girls before you go off and curl up next to your keyboard for the next two weeks?"

"Ha ha. Very funny." Richard stooped his large frame under the tree and kissed his wife on her cheek and his daughter on her head and went back inside. Naomi fingered the book while rubbing Brittany's tiny head, running her fingers through the baby's white fluff of hair. She opened the notebook and read.

Thursday, April 19, 1984, 5:00 P.M. American time:

On the plane heading toward the unknown. Okay, not really. Heading to Frankfurt. It's finally hit me that I'm really going. Alone. At last. I guess I've been numb to it all along. But now the feeling is settling in. I am going to land in Germany, and nobody will be there to meet me. I don't know a single person in Europe.

For reasons beyond my own rational comprehension I am choosing to travel through Europe alone. I am twenty-three years old and very inexperienced at traveling solo. I will stick to it, even though my overly-worried, overly-protective parents have offered to pay for an "18–35" tour that promises to help people older than eighteen and younger than thirty-five discover Europe from inside a crowded bus. Living with my parents and having a curfew again has been confining enough. (Leaving behind Scott is more of a relief than I ever imagined.)

I want adventure. After eighteen years of indoor education, I feel it is time to discover the secret knowledge of the world outside my own secure one. I will organize my own tour.

I bought a round-trip ticket to Frankfurt, but Greece is to be my first destination. I know Greece will be warmer. An airline ticket to the historic islands is too expensive, so I figure I will fly cheap and head south immediately. In fact, this is the only plan I have. I will let fate plan the rest.

With warm weather in mind I have somehow packed three pairs of shorts, a bathing suit, two pairs of blue jeans, four T-shirts, two Oxford button-down shirts, a pair of stylish pants, a brown cotton blazer, pairs of suede boots, topsiders, and leather sandals, eight pairs of underwear and two pairs of socks into my backpack. Knowing I would have no iron, Mom insisted I pack as much polyester as possible.

I squished a few essentials—toothbrush, vitamins, aspirin, shampoo, and whatnot—into side pockets. I am not too worried about replacing my ten tampons; girls, after all, bleed everywhere.

I'm bringing along a sleeping bag, which should come in mighty handy for overnight train trips and for something to lie on while roaming the Greek Isles on board ferries.

I have a twenty-three-dollar-a-day allowance. Twenty-three for a twenty-three-year-old. Totally appropriate, no? Everyone says I will run out of money halfway through my trip, but I am undeterred. I am in search of adventure by myself, for as long as I can, no matter what the cost.

Lastly, I am bringing this notebook. A journal. I take it for two reasons: one because I imagine myself sitting in cafes, drinking coffee, and writing about my surroundings the way Hemingway or others might have. The image is dramatic, romantic. The other reason is for my grandchildren. I envision them sitting in a moldy attic fifty years from now reading Grandma's journal of her trip alone through western Europe way back in the 1980s. I like the immortal ring to it.

I leave with a curiosity marked by eagerness and a naïve trust. I want to be open to everything; open-hearted, open-eyed, open-armed. I departed America smiling, and while I am in Europe, I hope most of the people will smile back.

"It's a travel journal. Wow," Naomi said, looking at her daughter, now fast asleep, a fist tucked under her tiny chin. "I should find out whose it is and call, huh? I mean, that would be the proper thing to do." She got up and lifted the baby into her arms, careful not to wake her. After tucking the little nugget into her crib, Naomi traipsed down to Richard's office, which took up fully one half of the bottom floor of their three-story house overlooking Lake Sammamish. She came up behind him and blew on his neck as he sat staring at his monitor.

"Cut it out, honey. I'm working."

"Yeah, and I'm flirting with my gorgeous husband. Listen," she said as she threw herself onto the leather couch across from his desk. "It's someone's travel journal. And it's old. Like from 1984. She was twenty-three, only a year older than me, and she took off to travel Europe by herself. Isn't that cool?"

"Actually, yes it is. Are you jealous? Do you wish it could have been you? Is that what you're saying?" Richard continued typing, more assiduously than before.

"You are so paranoid. No, I'm just saying . . . I don't know what I'm saying. I feel bad reading it. It is someone's private journal."

"Just give her a call and tell her, oops, sorry, we bought your diary for the price of fifty albums by mistake. Here it is. No harm done."

"I would, but there's no name or address in it. Just

names of friends who she wrote to while on her trip." Naomi looked behind her and watched a sailboat float by the window.

Richard looked up. "Call one of them. Any one of them would know her. Now, if you don't mind, sweetie . . ."

"Yeah, yeah. Work work work. Maybe we can have dinner together tonight?"

"Can't, love of my life. Meeting with Jim in Redmond. Talking to the big guys at Microsoft next week. Got to be on top of things. Tomorrow, though. Promise," Richard said, and picked up the phone as he blew her a kiss good-bye.

Naomi took the notebook into the den, where she lit the gas fireplace, laughing as she turned the switch and saw the pale, almost surreal yellowish flames burst up and over the blackened fake logs. Growing up, there was always a cord or two of split drying pine stacked up in the woodshed. Friends and extended family came to cut their own warmth from the Forest Service land that surrounded their property. As she swept her small body across the beige Berber carpeting on the floor she pretended for the moment that the hissing of the gas jets was really a crackling log igniting sparks and puffs of air. She grabbed a pillow from the couch and turned to the page where she left off.

Friday, April 20, 1984, in Rothenburg, Germany:

Almost sunset in one of the most beautiful villages ever seen. Cobblestone streets shaped in starfish patterns. A long-ago fortress set against the Rhine River. It's exactly 6:00 and I'm sitting in the village square listening to and watching the chimes ring in the village church.

Observation: Germans wear their wedding rings on their right hand and engagement rings on their left.

I'm hungry, but nobody speaks English, so I don't know how to order. I should try or starve to death.

11:00 P.M., German time:

Still Rothenburg and still nice . . . if not nicer. Went strolling and found a romantic outdoor cafe. Saw two semi-gorgeous boys and asked if either spoke English. Both did and they invited me to join them for coffee. We walked the streets and Thomas and Folka took me to a restaurant. I ate very strong cheese mixed with onions and spices and rye bread and drank thick German beer. They walked me back to the youth hostel, which I remembered being fine when I checked in this afternoon. But it had since turned into a home for the not-so-weary, but very hyper traveler. Five sets of bunk beds crammed into one little room. Open-doored showers and foul-smelling toilets turned this haven for the broke traveler into a place to go if "you really need a place to stay for under $10." Well, I left and got a private room in a nice hotel for $25. So much for $23 a day.

Saturday, 21 April, 9:30 A.M.:

Having breakfast in hotel. Lovely rolls with two strong cheeses, a hard-boiled egg, strawberry preserves, honey, butter and a pot of coffee. The city is alive and bustling very early. I got about five hours sleep last night, as Thomas and Folka knocked on my door after midnight and stayed telling me their life stories until 3:00.

An old man just came and sat at my table. He speaks no English and a little French (glad for that one year of French in 7th grade). It took us about ten minutes to realize we couldn't communicate too well. No matter. Ah, to be far from home, but to feel at home. Can she find her way in this maze? A smile can truly save civilization.

Naomi got up and stretched her back, reached with her arms side to side. Since having Brittany, her normally flexible back stiffened more quickly. But of all the women she knew since moving here, she had the only body that wasn't complained about on a constant basis. Petite and muscular, Naomi had no need for diets or indoor tennis. A little more mountain climbing would do, though. If not for the legs, then for the spirit.

She went into the kitchen, cleaned that morning by Carmen, and made herself a salad. She'd wake Brittany in a few minutes to feed her and give her a bath, bubbles and floating ducks, giggles and screams of delight. Her and Brittany's favorite time of the day. She munched on the salad—tomatoes and cucumbers, feta cheese and sunflower seeds speckled throughout bitter arugula leaves—and flipped through the red book that sat on the kitchen table.

28 April, Venice, Italy:

And so they come from miles around . . . Nice nap. Cold water on the face, brush hair, throw on a pair of jeans and off to the land of Venetians. Sitting at an outdoor cafe´ drinking espresso. Many people walking by. I must find food soon. Always hungry when the streets smell like pizza.

An old man took a picture of me when I bent down in an alleyway to pet a stray cat. Many young people in love here. I still remain a young American girl not in love, not strolling the streets hand in hand with my lover, not being romanced while floating dreamily in a gondola.

4:00: And so a day spent in Venice walking and sitting and walking and sitting and . . . My feet hurt, my eyes are tired of watching. Now I'm in a cafe on the waterfront. Nice sea breeze. Haven't spoken a word in three hours.

"How's the trip so far?" Richard asked as he stuck his fingers into the salad and grabbed a clump of oily leaves. He sat in front of her, put his elbows on the table, and stared into her eyes. "You look lost in thought. What's the baby doing?"

"Sleeping. I'll go wake her after travel girl leaves Italy. She had a nice time in Germany with some athletes. Then in Italy she met a stupid American guy from Wake Forest University who's studying art history there. He brought her along with some of the other students for a dinner out. She orders a huge plate of fried squid for the table, there's like eight other students, and she's munching away and notices no one is touching any of it. So she asks, 'What, no one likes squid?' and the others just look at her like she's from Mars and finally one of them tells her that it's impolite to eat from another person's plate! Is that sick or what? Here she flies halfway around the world to find a bunch of dumb polite Americans."

"What'd she do?" Richard wondered as he grabbed an Odwalla orange juice from the refrigerator and sat again.

"Left them after dinner and vowed to stay away from other Americans if at all possible. It's so weird, honey, how she can go for days without talking to anyone and it doesn't seem scary at all. She finds rooms really easily just by wandering the streets and people are so nice to her even if they don't understand a word she's saying." Naomi closed the book, took three gulps of the pulpy tangy juice, and went off to get Brittany.

Later that night Richard came home and found Naomi in bed with her legs up under the covers with the red booklet resting open against them. "Still traveling with your friend?"

"Jeez. What time is it?" She rolled over to look at the

clock on Richard's side of the bed. "It's after one. Why didn't you call?"

"Did you actually notice that I wasn't home?" Richard asked while he took off his clothes.

Naomi closed the book and puffed up the pillows behind her head. "No, not really. I'm totally into reading this. I should call one of those people tomorrow or drive out to her house and return the book to her, but I want to see what happens first."

Richard got into the king-sized bed and moved his large body next to Naomi's. "Where is the world traveler now?"

"Greece. She took this amazing boat trip where she slept out on the deck because all the cabins were taken. She slept in her sleeping bag at the bottom of the empty pool to be away from people and when she woke up, she climbed the ladder just as the sun was rising above the island mountains. Sounds pretty beautiful."

"Yeah, what else?" Richard yawned.

"Well, she had a nice time in Athens even though it was overrun with tourists and the Acropolis was being renovated, so it was a little disappointing to see scaffolding all over it. But some local businessman flirted with her and took her out for dinner. She was bummed because here she was in Greece and they ate Indian food."

"A free meal is a free meal if you're on a budget."

"That's so funny. She said the exact same thing. Any-

way, she didn't know which island to visit but met this guy—
she attracts guys like she's one of those sticky flypaper strips—
who asks her for help writing a letter in English to a friend in
America. He told her to go to this little village on the island
of Crete. It took forever, first on a boat, then a long bus ride
over the mountains, but she found this beautiful little fishing
village. She stayed in a room with a double bed overlooking
the Mediterranean. She had dinner with the family who owns
the place and it was, wait, here it is. 'Last night the woman who
owns the pension had me sit down in her little kitchen next
to a huge drum of olive oil (no Greek kitchen could ever be
without!). She fried some soft delicious calamari her husband
had just caught that morning, a fresh salad loaded with red
ripe sweet tomatoes, bread, stuffed grape leaves, homemade
family fruit wine, and some wonderful sugared cake. While I
ate, she, her husband, and their son, and I talked. I know
maybe ten Greek words now and they maybe fifteen English
words, yet we managed to voice our opinions on Reagan, Sta-
lin, solar energy, war, Hitler, school and island life. After
dinner I was shown the family album. I paid them $2, thanked
them abundantly (*efhahristow*) and went into town.' "

"Two bucks for that? 1984 was a good year for the
American dollar, I tell you," Richard said. He turned off his
light and rolled over in a fetal position with his back to his
wife.

• • •

She'd had the journal for two days and was starting to feel jitters of guilt. She was sitting in a pub in downtown Madison Park, the little neighborhood across Lake Washington. The inside was smoky and young university students were playing darts and drinking beer. A baseball game was on the television perched above her. She liked coming here, feeling a little closer to the life she had imagined she would have lived if not for her father swerving to avoid another car that had lost control on Highway 20, and going over a steep embankment. If not for meeting Richard. If not for Brittany, the little love of her life who came too soon, but was so welcome.

Richard didn't know she'd left the baby with a sitter; he didn't like anyone watching her. He was even a little distrustful of their only baby-sitter, Meagan, the teenage girl down the street who belonged to their club. But he wouldn't be home for dinner tonight and it felt good to be away from the quiet of the house, the soft lap of the tiny wavelets on their dock, and have a pub beer like any other twenty-two-year-old on a Saturday afternoon. She wondered if travel girl felt the same when she was sitting in cafés and restaurants, being looked at by unfamiliar faces because she was alone. The mix of fright, vulnerability, and independence was invigorating to Naomi. She wondered if she would want to continue on for-

ever like this, the way travel girl thought she would when she
wrote on her way back to Italy.

I think I want to travel forever. All sorts; backpacking, luxury, moun-
tains, resorts, paradises, cities. I am going to work for a while at home,
buy a horse and horseback through Canada next. And after that, more
work and a trip to the South Pacific. How can I really settle down into
a job or a career or a family when there is so much to see?

Naomi took a bite of her Chinese chicken salad and
imagined herself in a small café in Italy, under the shade of a
striped awning, writing in her own diary. Baseball faded into
the background.

15 May, 12:30 P.M.*:*

Well, I'm still in Arona, glorious lake city surrounded by the Italian
Alps and smelling like the sweet wisteria that overgrows itself around the
lattice of my deck. After a night of discoing with five nice Italian boys,
I sat in the small hotel lobby and sipped Amaretto while reading my
Lawrence Sanders book. A beautiful young man sat across from me and
began speaking Italian. I listened politely, nodding a few times, then
laughed and told him I wasn't Italian. He immediately switched to perfect
English. Roberto was schooled in England and worked on cruise ships
in the Caribbean. He now owns a shoe factory. We went to my room

and watched a Clark Gable movie in Italian, then a samurai movie. He begged me to stay a few days more in Arona.

Woke this morning early and while Roberto went on sales calls, I went to the town's flea market. They sell everything: cheese, meats, fish, plants, clothes. Not as nice as the one in Florence. I bought some Brie, bread, and marinated octopus and had a little picnic by the lake with the pigeons. I really enjoy my times alone. I speak so little these days, new for me. I realized how grand it was to be traveling alone when I went into St. Peter's Basilica in Rome. Had someone been beside me I would have felt the need to say, "Wow, isn't this beautiful?" But because I was alone, I could comment only to myself. Take in everything around me in a complete, whole, selfish way. When I am alone I feel alive, vibrant, inquisitive, friendly. I watch my step. I am aware of the signs of life around me. I am vulnerable and anxious. When I am with others, I feel safe, secure. I am not as willing to look, to find adventure. I become lazy. Observation: At train stations you can buy wine from vendors who pass bottles right through the open train windows to you.

The bar erupted in a cacophony of shouts and hoots. Naomi looked up from the book for a moment, took another bite of salad, let her eyes wander over the dark interior, smoke and noise wafting in and out of sunlight shafts, and nodded her head again.

If we are all constantly searching for that someone who is to make us fulfilled, will we ever be truly fulfilled alone? Does man or woman actually need another to satisfy his or her life? I think the real reason I came here is to find true love. I want so much to find someone who I can explore this world with. Yet I want to be so in love with myself that other people are not needed. I cannot figure out how to be truly satisfied with myself.

Naomi thought about this question of need as she picked past the dry chicken and went digging for the crunchy noodles and mandarin orange morsels hidden on the bottom of the fake wooden bowl. Of course I needed Richard to make me happy, she thought. Where was my life going; a storeroom of guilt—she should be doing more for her mother. And sadness. God, how she missed her father, strong, silent, and always smiling through the dust of his beard. And empty hope; how would she have ever made a life for herself if she couldn't even get a college scholarship? But Richard came along and all plans for making it on her own faded behind the voice in her head telling her to reach for the solid hand he was offering.

Here was this girl, exploring the wilds of a new place and what is she wondering about? Self-happiness. Love. As she drove across the I-90 bridge toward home Naomi fretted for a moment that she had never known such trite loves as travel girl knew. Yet, here she was saying that now that she's had all these brief and unrestrained love affairs, what she wants is honest love.

At least travel girl got to see the other side of the heart, the frivolous and uncaring side of passion, Naomi realized with a stab of envy as she pulled into her circular driveway. She extended her childhood by playing with boys, lining them up like soldiers in a muddy backyard. No one would die from such deeds. All in a day's fun. Naomi never graduated from dolls, pretty in their embroidery and ribbons. As she opened the tall stately wooden front door framed on the top border with teal and opaque stained glass, she knew she never would.

Meagan was watching television in the den when Naomi walked in and stood silently for a moment behind the couch, looking at the seventeen-year-old. She had the channel changer in her hand and was flipping back and forth between a cooking show and some vile gang movie on TBS. All the choices were laid out before her like some unearthed jewels on a sandy beach. A rare and ultimately underutilized gem, youth is, she thought. I hope she does more with hers than I did with mine.

Naomi coughed and Meagan jumped up from the couch. She apologized for lounging about but said Brittany went down a few minutes ago and she was bored by her homework.

Naomi laughed. "That's fine, sweetie. Did she give you any fuss?"

"Nah, she's a perfect child. We played a little and then she yawned, so I put her down, read her a few lines from my history book, and she was out like a light in five minutes."

"You want a juice or something?" Naomi hoped Meagan would not rush off so fast; she felt like being in someone's company. "Britty and I made some delicious chocolate chip cookies yesterday."

"Uh, I know. Your husband came home an hour ago and shared a few with me."

"Richard's home? Why are you still here, then?"

"No, he ate a cookie and said he had to get back to Redmond. But I'd be happy to have another one. They're yummy."

Naomi flushed. "Oh, good. Come on, then." The girls went into the kitchen and Naomi poured them each a glass of cold milk and set out the plate of cookies, still chewy. "So, Meagan, are you still thinking of going on that teen tour through Europe next summer?" Naomi asked.

"Yup. Been saving my money. If you notice it's Saturday evening and I'm here instead of at the mall with my friends."

"That's so funny. I mean I've been reading this travel journal of, uh, a friend of mine who did the same thing. Stayed home on weekends. Worked and saved enough to make the trip."

"Wow. Can I read it or talk to her in person? I bet she has some great advice," Meagan said, then gulped the milk down.

"Well, I don't know. She gave it to me in confidence, you know?" Naomi lied and felt like such a jerk. "I could talk to her and see if she'd get together with you or something. We'll see, okay?"

"Sure."

"You know, I've been reading it for days and thinking how jealous I was of her going off on her own like that—"

"She went alone?"

"Oh, yes. But she was twenty-three when she went. A whole lot different than seventeen. I think joining a tour group is a great way to see Europe. Anyway, she just got dumped by this fabulous guy she met in Italy and now she's rethinking the whole travel thing."

Meagan reached for another cookie. "What happened? I love the juicy details."

"About the guy? Well, she met him in this little Italian resort and they had a pretty romantic time. But she wanted to travel some more, so they agreed to meet back in Italy in about a month. First she goes to Paris and visits the Louvre. She climbed the steps up to the top of Notre Dame. You know, the church?"

"I'm definitely going to do that."

Naomi nodded in consent and continued. "She was on

this meager budget and she stayed in the cheapest place she could find. All night there were people coming and going and so much noise, she couldn't sleep. So she gets up and goes downstairs and finds out she's staying in a hotel where prostitutes take their customers!"

"No way, Jose! Now, that sounds like a nightmare." Meagan scratched her arm. "What else happened?"

"She goes to Monte Carlo and sees the big castle there and meets this girl from New Orleans, what's her name, Sue Ann. The two of them go to Spain together and have a great time. They go to the Alhambra in Granada. Meagan, you have to go there. The gardens sound amazing. Red poppies, flowers galore. A perfect picnic spot.

"Anyway, this Sue Ann turns out to be a total party girl and mooch. She goes out every night and brings men back with her to their hotel rooms. My friend lends her money and she promises to repay her when they go to Italy, where Sue Ann is living for the year. The train trip back to Italy from the coast of Spain is a nightmare. The train derailed and they were stuck in the middle of nowhere for hours. It took them fifty hours to get to Venice and just when they got off the train after this awful trip, Sue Ann disappears into a crowd and my friend is left alone, never to get her money back."

"Total drag. What a wench. Maybe your friend was a bit too trusting." Meagan sat up straight in the wicker kitchen chair.

"You can say that again. The whole time she's gone, she's been sending postcards to this Italian guy. She's fantasizing about actually marrying him and living in Italy. She forgets all about Sue Ann and makes her way to this town just outside Venice where he lives. She ended up sleeping in the train station because all the hotels were booked and she couldn't get a hold of him on the telephone.

"She finally talks to a friend of his on the telephone who picks her up at the train station and takes her to his house where this Roberto guy is going to meet her. Hold on, I've got to read what she says." Naomi fished the journal out of her leather daypack and sat back down.

" 'Tuesday, June 12, 1:30 P.M. I combed my hair as my heart raced anxiously. I never stopped wanting to see Roberto. I conjured up such romantic daydreams and imagined a deep love affair. I pictured our meeting again as intense. But when that gorgeous Italian man rode up on his Yamaha 600, stepped off, and looked at me, I knew once again that my idealistic mind had made up a fairy tale. He hugged me hello and the first thing out of his mouth was, "You cut your hair." And oh God, he looked so beautiful standing there. My heart was breaking into little pieces when he moved forward to make room for me on his bike. We rode through the green countryside, me behind that incredible body with his thick brown hair flying in the breeze. We stopped at the old palace of the king of Venezia. A majestic building surrounded by about 300 acres of dense forest and rose gardens and fountains and towers. No one lives there now. We hiked the grounds as Roberto told me about how he had fallen for a sad French girl and how he can no longer love me. And the worst part is that he met her only a few days after I left, at the same hotel where we met.' "

Meagan sighed. "Gosh. What a bummer. What else?"

Naomi closed the sacred book, not wanting Meagan to even have a glance at the handwriting. She'd become possessive of the memoir, hoarding its secrets as if her own. She knew she'd be driving to West Seattle the next day to return the lost words to travel girl.

"They hung out with his friends for a couple of days. She helped stuff homemade sausage, went to a sailboat regatta, ate loads of good food. Her favorite was tortellini carbonara, and after Roberto told his mother that, she made it for her every night. Then she said good-bye and took a train to Germany."

"Lost love is so sad. I'm glad I don't have anyone in my life right now. Boyfriends are hard work. I sort of like the idea that there could be someone perfect out there that I haven't met yet." Meagan smiled as her head tilted slightly to one side. Her posture was perfect and her white teeth gleamed with promise. Naomi hated her for just a second.

She got up and put the glasses in the sink. "Yes, but you should be careful not to jump at the first good offer. Like my friend said, it might seem like the right one, but there's always the chance some French girl is waiting around the corner."

Meagan laughed and got up from the table. "You're funny, Naomi. You don't have to worry about me. I'd never think of marrying the first man who entered my life. I want to live a long time alone, doing what I want to do, before getting swept off my feet and into some big house on the lake like my mom did."

"You mean like I did."

"What? No, I didn't mean to . . ." Meagan stuttered and a blush rose, darkening her young pink cheeks.

Naomi smiled and put her arm around the girl. "I'm kidding. How much do I owe you?"

It was cloudy and threatening to rain the next day. Naomi zipped Brittany into a blue-and-red fleece suit and they took off toward the edge of Seattle, where ferry boats and whales often cross the same paths. She pulled up in front of the weathered house, amazed at her memory for finding it again so easily. She didn't remember the person or people who were selling their junk, but she remembered looking into the front windows while browsing the items for sale along the sidewalk out front. There was a beautiful collection of seashells atop a tiny shelf running the length of a wall. She glanced in the window now and saw tacky plates with place names balanced precariously along the same shelf.

Naomi knew instinctively that travel girl no longer lived here. She and her shells had taken the money from the yard sale and vamoosed into a new sunset. But she had to be sure. She left Brittany strapped in and hurried up the three stairs to the front door and knocked. The wind came off Puget Sound in a rush and whipped at her back. A middle-aged woman wearing a stained apron opened the door.

"Hi," Naomi said. "I was at a garage sale here last summer and I bought something by mistake from the owner. Is there a young woman who still lives here?"

"Nope. This was a rental house. Lots of young people lived here. But now it's mine. It was my brother's. He died. So I live here."

Naomi looked over her shoulder and spied Brittany fingering the plastic key ring attached to her car seat. "Any chance you'd have a forwarding address from the last tenant so I could find her?"

"Threw all that out." The woman appeared to snort. A telephone rang behind her. "If you'll excuse me." She closed the door.

There were numerous names and addresses and phone numbers on the inside cover of the diary, but the names Jerry and

Helen Fisher appeared first. Naomi guessed they might be travel girl's parents, so she dialed their number first.

"Hello?" A woman's voice, maternal and soft.

"Yes, is this Mrs. Fisher?"

A slight suspicion arose. "Can I help you?"

Naomi went on. "I know this is sort of strange, but do you have a daughter or sister maybe who went traveling in Europe back in 1984?"

"Yes, that's my daughter, Elly. Wait. You found her diary. Thank God."

Elly. A name fell upon a featureless face. "I did. You see, we, my husband and I bought some albums at a garage sale last summer and we only just got around to—"

"Of course, the garage sale. She's been going crazy, you know. She could not figure out how she lost that one thing in the move. I've got to call her right away. Give me your number."

Naomi hesitated for a moment. "Uh. Oh. Is she still in Seattle?" she asked finally.

"Yes. Yes, she's still living there."

"Why don't you give me her number then."

Naomi detected some doubt, but the woman obviously thought better of it. Just protecting her young. Naomi could relate. "Even better," Elly's mother said. "She's staying with some friends, Vanessa and Mark. You'll call right away?"

She took the phone number and promised to call immediately. The woman thanked her and they hung up.

She stood by Richard's desk, gazing out the window to the lake beyond and the white-tipped Cascades farther still. The red journal stared up at her from the glazed brown desk next to the black phone. There were still a few more pages, a few more adventures to follow. Dare she do it now? Now that travel girl was Elly, a living woman who longed for a lost book? She picked up the receiver.

"Hello? This is Naomi Kimmich. I've got your travel journal."

Gasps of happiness erupted in the sounds of laughter. "Yippee! How did you find it? Where was it?" The girl was blissful and it was contagious. Naomi told her about the garage sale and how Richard just this week found the journal and since there was no name on it, she didn't know what to do, but Richard told her to call the names in the book, and well, here they are.

"Did you read it?"

The question shook the air from Naomi's lungs. She was completely dumbfounded; to lie or not to lie? "Well, I did skim it a little, but not the whole thing. I'm sorry if—"

"Don't be," came the voice, now twelve years older than the voice in the book, the voice that had kept company with Naomi these last few days. "I don't mind at all. I wrote it so someone would read it, my kids or grandchildren, whoever. I suppose other than my family, who I was forced to read it to when I got back, no one else will."

"I really enjoyed the parts I read, Elly. It sounds as if

you had the time of your life. I'm slightly jealous of you, you know."

"Go on! No need to be jealous of some spoiled girl's trip through Europe. You know it's easier to travel there than America. I mean safer, cheaper. Anyway, can we get together so I can have it? What are you doing tomorrow?"

Naomi didn't know what to say. She didn't know if she wanted to meet travel girl, see her face-to-face. She didn't understand why, but she wanted to keep the distance alive. "I can just put it in the mail. What's your address?"

"Nah. Don't mail it. My husband and I are leaving for Africa next week. We're at our friends' house and everything is in storage. It might get lost in the mail and I can't deal with losing it again before leaving."

Africa! She sounded so comfortable with herself, so much like the intrepid girl she was twelve years ago. Dynamic and even a little bossy. Naomi had to meet her. They agreed to meet at a Starbucks in Kirkland, noon tomorrow.

They sat on opposite sides of a picnic table bolted to the ground a few yards from the coffee shop. It was cool, but the wind was calm.

"I'm glad you read it. Makes me feel like the trip was real, not just some story I made up." Elly sipped her cappuccino through the hole in the plastic lid. She was younger-looking than Naomi pictured. And more slight. She had imagined a larger girl carrying all that backpack weight around the busy streets of Rome. She understood the attraction men must have felt for her; Naomi liked her the moment they met.

Elly leaned down and pulled Brittany out of the stroller and put her onto her lap. "You don't mind, do you? I'm sort of rehearsing, deciding if we want one." Brittany cooed past her pacifier and reached out to tug Elly's long brown hair. "When they're this cute, it's impossible to decide against it. You're awfully young to be a mother, if you don't mind me saying that."

"Twenty-two. I got married young. It was that or work and go to junior college. What am I saying?" Naomi sipped her hot chocolate and looked away.

"Twenty-two is the perfect age to try something new. For me it was going to Europe. For you it was giving birth. It's all relative." When the baby started to fuss, she handed Brittany across the table to Naomi, who kissed her daughter, placed her in the stroller, and handed her the stuffed Ernie to giggle against.

"You're going to Africa next week?"

"Yes. Me and my husband. We just got married. His name is Daniel. We've been working and saving our money. A lot like what I did twelve years ago. But I'm not going alone this time. This'll be our honeymoon."

"You're so lucky."

"I feel very lucky." Elly put on her wool gloves, leaned

her elbows onto the discolored redwood, and scanned the water's horizon. Naomi twisted in her seat and followed her gaze to the boats rocking against the dock. She turned back around after a moment.

"I guess you had a lot of other romances before you met the right guy."

"Skimmed it, huh? Yeah, you could say I slept my way around Europe, but I have no regrets, just lots of memories."

"That affair with Roberto broke my heart," Naomi admitted to Elly. "How long did it take you to get over it?"

"Is that where you left off? I got over it the moment I met Alex. Where did you stop reading?" Her fingers swerved across the table to the journal. Idly, she flipped the pages like one does when making those fake cartoons on the margins of paper come to life.

Naomi said, "Just as you were heading to Amsterdam."

"I stopped in Füssen, Germany, on the way to check out that famous castle, the one Disneyland used as the model for its magic castle. Only this one had real jeweled bedposts.

"I was walking down the street and I looked at this guy and he looked back and the next thing you know we're having coffee together. He was astounding. British officer on a training exercise with his troops. Green eyes, blond hair, and that accent. I love that accent."

"I know what you mean," said Naomi, once again captivated by travel girl's story.

Elly fingered her hair. "We spent two nights together there. He had to get back to his base, so I went to Austria." She broke out singing, "The hills are alive with the sound of music," and they both laughed.

"I met this nice guy, Franz—what else?—who took me all over the mountains and lakes. We had a blast. But I missed Alex, so I visited him where he was stationed in northern Germany. It was blissful. We talked about getting married. He talked about trying to get posted to America. Roberto was history. I was going to be the English Lieutenant's Woman."

"And?"

"I got back to the States and did nothing but pine for him. He wrote me amazing love letters. Here." She flipped to the back of the book. An envelope was taped to the binding. "This is the one he wrote right after I left him. Read it. I've got to pee."

Naomi hadn't realized there was an envelope in the diary. She felt awkward reading the letter, but Elly did insist. She had never gotten a love letter from anyone. She'd never loved and left. Richard had always called. She opened the envelope.

August 28, 1984

My Darling Elly,

It is now a week since I last saw you and life has been hell. I now deeply wish I had not let you leave.

The only thing I have to remind me of you are memories and your sunglasses. Even my photographs won't be back for at least another week. I really hope you write, as I will at least have a part of you then—albeit stretched over thousands of miles.

I think about you every second of the day and my heart seems to have something squeezing it. It is almost empty of love, as you now have it—I need you. I want you, but I am stuck in this godforsaken country—what to do? I have been trying to work out a time when I can go on holiday so that I can come and see you.

I am at a loss for words. I don't want to write to you, I want to hold you, be with you, touch you. I am frustrated to say the least. Nothing else appeals to me; no one else interests me. I have not rung any of my friends and I do not want to. Everywhere I look I just see and feel your face. I look at my watch, work out the time in California, and wonder what you're doing.

I have so many memories from so short a time. The smallest little thing like you putting stamps on a postcard or rolling my sleeves up or making me wish over an eyelash. I can remember it all.

It is now 0540 A.M.; I have to go, as I have a parade in a few minutes. I want you to know that you have taken a large part of me home with you and I would love you to hold it forever.

I love you,
Alex

"He really loved you." Naomi stared at Elly, who had just returned to the bench. "What happened?"

"Well." She twisted a loose thread from her jacket around her forefinger. "He visited me a few months later in San Diego. He looked so different in that setting. I can't really explain it, but the intrigue was gone. I have to say, everything in Europe was more romantic because it was in Europe. The relationship just sort of died after that."

"Just like that?" Naomi was surprised by her own defensiveness. In a way she envied her, but at the same time felt embarrassed for Elly. The girl had moved on from loving him as soon as he got on the airplane to leave. So many thousands of miles away. And in the end, nothing on the other side.

The sun came out from behind the clouds and splashed the lake water with glints of light. The women left their table and walked to the lake's edge. Naomi let Brittany crawl around on the ground.

"I know. I was young, what can I say? I treated him well, even though I had a lousy time with him. He never stopped drinking scotch and smoking cigarettes. And that high attitude. Fun guy, but he never gave that army officer routine a rest." She picked up a rock and threw it into the lake. For a moment she froze, remembering something. There was no way Naomi was going to ask her to share.

A cool breeze drifted off the lake where the million-dollar yachts heaved and groaned. Naomi watched the side of the girl's head. "You don't miss him still?"

"I miss the picture of us together. I liked the idea of being a British army wife. Hell, when I was at their base I got to ride on the polo ponies that they had there. And I had tea with some lord.

"I imagined my lace-inundated English country home smelling of lavender and peonies. And my polite children scurrying about the gardens with their nanny. I would hire Mary Poppins, of course."

Naomi laughed. "Of course." She watched Brittany grab at a muddy rock. "I know you won't mind me saying this, but you sort of lived in a dream world. I mean, you fantasized about life with different men, but real life, it never even came close to the fantasies." She watched Elly observe a young couple saunter by hand in hand, both not looking ahead, but at each other. The wind dared to whip the girl's hair into the boy's face, and for a moment he seemed annoyed as he picked it from his eyes.

"True. I'm done looking for love out there." Elly pointed to the west with both hands outstretched. "I found it right here in Seattle."

"He's obviously into traveling like you are. You said in your journal that you want to spend your life traveling."

"You never finished reading it, so you never got to the

bored cynical rant I wrote toward the end," Elly said. "I did say that at the beginning, and I felt that way. I felt alive in the cities. I waited for adventure to fall on me every time I got on another train. But after a while I felt a little bored by it all. Slightly underwhelmed." She turned to Naomi and her eyes brightened with enthusiasm. "You like to hike?"

"Oh my God, yes. I spent my whole life hiking the Sierras and I'm hoping to do a lot more in the Cascades."

Elly smiled and asked, "And what do you love most about it?"

Naomi reflected back to the walks she and her father and brother used to take in the Bowman Lakes Wilderness when the snow at the lower altitudes kept most folks home, warm. "The wildness. The complete and utter silence. I feel so alive when I'm surrounded by nature, you know?"

"I do know," Elly replied. "Here. 'July 14. Europe is riddled with people. I'm actually feeling bored with people and their dirty cities. One can only experience so much of being a tourist, taking trains, running from the rain. Travel is definitely work. It is hard physical labor to travel, it is wearing on the body and soul. No matter how wonderful the places you visit, staying in different hotel rooms every other day, looking for one, carrying a backpack, thirteen-hour train rides, wears on you.

" 'Traveling has made me yearn for two extremes—either to travel and share myself with the world forever out of the fear that if I don't, I will miss something vital, that I will rot away in one tiny city in one house in one country in one state, and when I die, I will be nothing more than a statistic, one less body walking around filling up minuscule space.

" 'The other feeling travel has brought on is the feeling of futility in trying to accomplish everything. When you're happy with who you are and just being alive, then it doesn't matter if the world ever gets to know you. Travel makes me see that people are exactly the same everywhere, and the cities are so much the same too. Sure, outward appearances, the superficial surfaces of the universe vary, mostly in sight. But what counts is all the same. I traveled to see variations in architecture, in churches, in coastlines, in valleys, and mountain ranges. The people do not surprise me.

" 'I am not a city girl. I know that the times I have truly felt glad to be a part of the human race, truly understood what self-satisfaction meant, were those times spent exploring nature. I do need the stimulation of cities, yes, but I have found that after spending a night on the town or a day hiking in the woods, I will always feel more alive from the day in the woods.

" 'I have still not seen beauty that matches that of Yosemite, the California deserts, the state of Utah, the northern California coastline, the rivers, the lakes, and the redwood forests. I am lucky to have been able to see all those natural works of art. My travels make me homesick for their awesome beauty.' "

"Wow." Naomi wasn't sure what to say. She liked the fact that Elly didn't find complete happiness in her travels, either in love or in adventure, but she wouldn't say that out loud.

"There you go." Elly closed the book and stuffed it into her black, blue, and purple Guatemalan purse. "You thought it was all fun and excitement, right?"

"You love the outdoors more than the foreign cities? You really missed being here?" Naomi was surprised by travel girl's pronouncements. She came here to return a lost book, but found a hint of vindication. "But you're going to Africa?"

"Sure. It's not like we can see herds of lions around here. Daniel and I really want to see that wilderness before it's all gone. We're hoping to climb Mount Kenya."

"I still want to go abroad someday."

"Then you should," Elly said, as she fished for her keys at the bottom of her bag. "Just don't assume you should be looking for something you can't find right here. Anyway, it was really nice to meet you. I'll give you a call sometime. Maybe we can get together again."

Naomi buckled her daughter into the stroller and watched Elly walk toward her parked car.

Richard came home late. Before going upstairs to check on his family, he headed down to his office to make a few notes about the meeting he had just come from. He threw off his leather jacket and switched on the brass desk lamp. As he reached for the computer mouse he saw a yellow sticky note stuck to the side of his monitor. He pulled it off and read it.

Richard,

It seems to me we haven't spent enough time exploring the great outdoors together. Brittany needs to learn that not all grass grows in neat rows. I am therefore requesting you to join your wife and daughter this Friday for a nice hike up to Annette Lake.

P.S. I love you and want to watch the stars in the night sky with you by my side, always.

Naomi

Richard smiled and reached over to his desk calendar, where he started flipping forward to Friday's page.

Acknowledgments

For his faith in me and this book from the very beginning, and the efforts he took on our behalf, I am eternally grateful to my friend, writer David Rensin. He not only showed me the door, but he opened it, and escorted me through. He gave unselfishly of his time, honesty, and vision. Indeed, his belief sustained me always. It is to David that I am most deeply indebted.

I greatly admire and adore Brian DeFiore, my literary representative, who took a chance on me. Brian serves as a patient sounding board, and he knows what matters in the big picture. I hope to have the pleasure of appreciating long into the future his laughter, remarkable intuition, and all-around chutzpah.

Thank you to the wonderful folks at Hyperion who offered assurances and benevolence: Laura Drew for her imagery; Ben Loehnen for the repartee and thoughtfulness; and to my editor, Leigh Haber, literary lodestar. I thank her for her instincts and her sensitivity. She made it easy for me to trust her; it helped that she was most often right.

More than a few friends and family either read the manuscript or offered me suggestions anyway, and I am ineffably grateful to all of them for their encouragement. Thanks to Mark S. Roy; Barbara Roemer; Marci Pliskin; Jennifer Ellen Goss; Robert Story; Judy Rosenthal; James Larkin; Jennifer New; Tracy Callaway; Sherie Maddox; Scott Young; Melissa Smith; Amy Luoma; Misha Renclair; Janet Cohen; and my inimitable mother, Florine Kusel.

I blow kisses to my brother, Scott Kusel, Computer Geeks, and Igor Zlimen for their technological generosity.

To Emily Eldridge, I bestow the honorary title "Friend Who Always Knew."

And finally, I offer loving thanks to my husband, Victor Prussack, and our baby daughter, Loy. Victor, I thank you for being indulgent, indefatigable, and wise; for being my best friend and fiercest ally; for holding me in your arms, kissing my eyes, and loving me absolutely. Without you and Loy to share it with, none of this would matter.